# Jude the Obscure

'We loved each other too much, too selfishly, you and I, Jude; and now we're punished . . .'

Young Jude Fawley lives in the sleepy village of Marygreen. But he often looks across the fields to the shiny roofs and tall buildings of the city of Christminster. One day, he promises himself, he will leave obscurity in Marygreen and go there. He will study at the university, enter the Church and become a great man.

But it is not easy for a poor boy to follow the path Jude has chosen, and life has many surprises for him. First there is Arabella Donn, the beautiful country girl who is looking for a husband. And then there is Sue Bridehead, whom he loves.

And soon Jude is learning what it is like to follow your heart in a world where it can be dangerous to have dreams – and to be too different from the crowd.

Thomas Hardy was one of the greatest British novelists of the nineteenth century, and his books are still very popular today.

He was born in 1840 in a village in Dorset, England. He trained as an architect, but always loved literature, and wrote his first novel in 1867. But it was only after *Far from the Madding Crowd*, in 1874, that he was able to give up architecture and live by writing. In the following years he wrote many novels and short stories which were well-received, but *Tess of the d'Urbervilles* (1891) and *Jude the Obscure* (1896) shocked readers of the time. His attitudes towards men and women and marriage did not seem 'respectable'. After *Jude the Obscure*, Hardy stopped writing novels and concentrated on poetry.

All Hardy's novels are about the people of the west of England, where he was born and grew up. He gave imaginary names to towns and gave the whole area the name of 'Wessex', which was its real name centuries ago.

You can also read *Under the Greenwood Tree* and *Far from the Madding Crowd* by Thomas Hardy in Penguin Readers.

D0313635

## OTHER TITLES IN THE SERIES

The following titles are available at Levels 4, 5 and 6:

*Level 4*
The Boys from Brazil
The Breathing Method
The Burden of Proof
The Client
The Danger
Detective Work
The Doll's House and Other Stories
Dracula
Far from the Madding Crowd
Farewell, My Lovely
Glitz
Gone with the Wind, Part 1
Gone with the Wind, Part 2
The House of Stairs
The Locked Room and Other Horror
    Stories
The Lost World
The Mill on the Floss
The Mosquito Coast
The Picture of Dorian Gray
Seven
Strangers on a Train
White Fang

*Level 5*
The Baby Party and Other Stories
The Body
The Firm
The Grass is Singing
The Old Jest
The Pelican Brief
Pride and Prejudice
Prime Suspect
Sons and Lovers
A Twist in the Tale
The Warden
Web

*Level 6*
The Edge
The Long Goodbye
Misery
The Moonstone
Mrs Packletide's Tiger and Other
    Stories
Presumed Innocent
A Tale of Two Cities
The Thorn Birds
Wuthering Heights

For a complete list of the titles available in the Penguin Readers series please write to the following address for a catalogue: Penguin ELT Marketing Department, Penguin Books Ltd, 27 Wrights Lane, London W8 5TZ.

# *Jude the Obscure*

## THOMAS HARDY

Level 5

Retold by Katherine Mattock
Series Editor: Derek Strange

PENGUIN BOOKS

## PENGUIN BOOKS

Published by the Penguin Group
Penguin Books Ltd, 27 Wrights Lane, London W8 5TZ, England
Penguin Books USA Inc., 375 Hudson Street, New York, New York 10014, USA
Penguin Books Australia Ltd, Ringwood, Victoria, Australia
Penguin Books Canada Ltd, 10 Alcorn Avenue, Toronto, Ontario, Canada M4V 3B2
Penguin Books (NZ) Ltd, 182–190 Wairau Road, Auckland 10, New Zealand

Penguin Books Ltd, Registered Offices: Harmondsworth, Middlesex, England

*Jude the Obscure* was first published in 1896
This adaptation published by Penguin Books 1993
4 6 8 10 9 7 5

Illustrations by Chris Chaisty

Printed in England by Clays Ltd, St Ives plc
Set in 11/13pt Lasercomp Bembo

## *To the teacher:*

In addition to all the language forms of Levels One to Four, which are used again at this level of the series, the main verb forms and tenses used at Level Five are:

- present simple verbs with future meaning, further continuous forms, further passive forms and conditional clauses (using the 'third' or 'unfulfilled past' conditional)
- modal verbs: *may* (to express permission and make requests), *will have*, *must have* and *can't have* (to express assumptions) and *would rather* (to state preferences).

Specific attention is paid to vocabulary development in the Vocabulary Work exercises at the end of the book. These exercises are aimed at training students to enlarge their vocabulary systematically through intelligent reading and effective use of a dictionary.

## *To the student:*

Dictionary Words:

- As you read this book, you will find that some words are in darker black ink than the others on the page. Look them up in your dictionary, if you do not already know them, or try to guess the meaning of the words first, and then look them up later, to check.

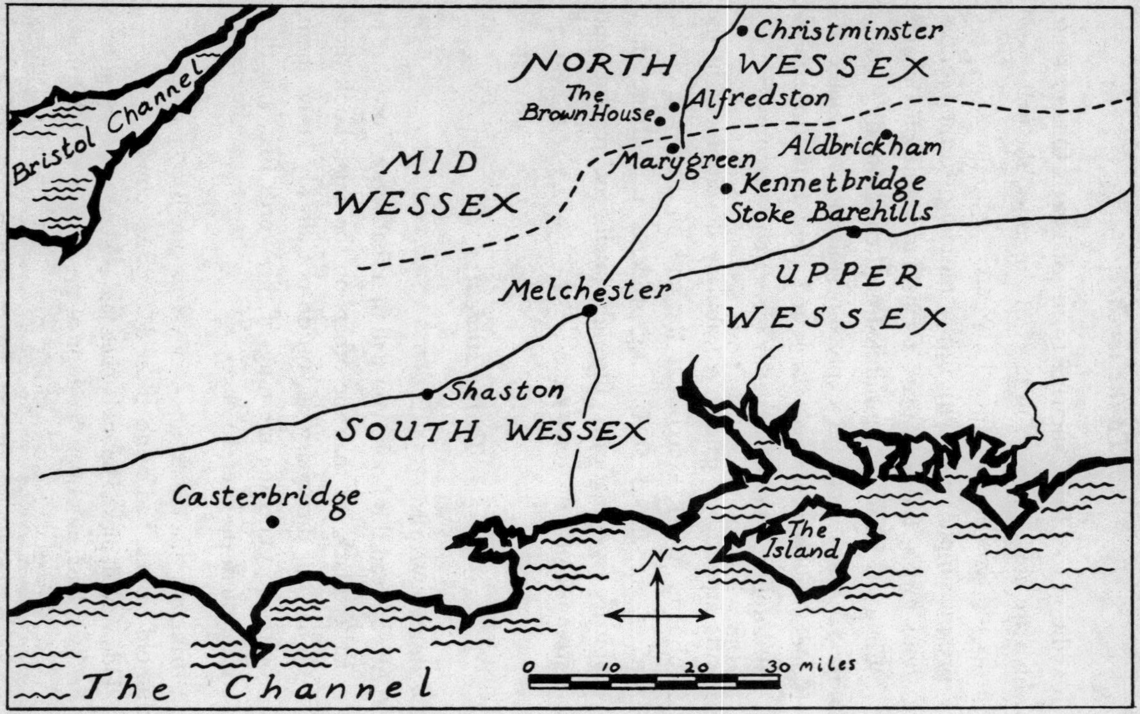


*Map of Hardy's Wessex (the names of places are imaginary)*

# Chapter One

The schoolmaster was leaving the village and everybody seemed sorry. As his belongings were brought out of the schoolhouse, tears came into the eyes of a small boy of eleven, one of his night-school pupils.

'Why are you going to Christminster, Mr Phillotson?' asked the boy.

'You wouldn't understand, Jude,' the schoolmaster said kindly. 'You will, perhaps, when you are older.'

'I think I would understand now, Mr Phillotson.'

'Well then,' said the teacher. 'I'm going to Christminster to be near the university. My dream is to go to university and then to enter the Church.'

Jude helped to lift Phillotson's things onto a **cart**, all except a piano. 'Aunt can look after that,' the boy suggested, 'until you send for it.'

At nine o'clock, the schoolmaster got up into the cart beside his box of books. 'Goodbye, my friends,' he said. 'Be a good boy, Jude. Be kind to animals and read all you can. And if you ever come to Christminster, hunt me out.'

The horse and cart moved off across the village green, past the **well** and the old **cottages** and the new church. Jude looked sadly down into the well at the water far below. 'He was too clever to stay here any longer,' he said to himself. 'A small, sleepy village like Marygreen!'

'Bring me that water, you lazy young good-for-nothing!' A thin old woman had come to the door of her cottage.

Jude waved, picked up his buckets and walked across the green.

A little blue sign over the door of the cottage said, 'Drusilla Fawley, **baker**'. This was Jude's great-aunt, his grandfather's sister. As he emptied the buckets, he could hear her talking inside to some of the other village women.

'And who's *he*?' asked a newcomer when Jude entered.

'My great-nephew,' replied Miss Fawley. 'He came up to me from South Wessex a year ago, when his father died. Poor useless boy! But he has to earn a penny wherever he can. Just now, he keeps the birds away for Farmer Troutham.'

'And he can help you with the baking, I suppose.'

'Hmph!' said Miss Fawley. 'It's a pity the schoolmaster didn't take him with him to Christminster. The boy's crazy for books. His cousin Sue's the same, I've heard, though I've hardly seen her since her mother – well, I won't go into that. Jude,' she said, turning to him, 'don't *you* ever marry. The Fawleys shouldn't marry.'

Jude went out to the bakehouse and ate the cake put out for his breakfast. Then he climbed over a **hedge** onto a path that led down to a large, lonely field planted with crops.

Clackety-clack. Clackety-clack. Every few seconds, the boy banged together two pieces of wood to frighten the birds away. Then, feeling tired and sorry for them, he threw down the clacker. 'Farmer Troutham can afford to let you have *some* dinner,' he said aloud. 'Eat, my dear little birdies!' The birds, black shapes on the brown earth, stayed and ate.

WHAM-CLACK! Jude and the birds rose together into the air as a red-faced farmer hit the boy on the seat of his trousers with his own clacker. 'So!' shouted Troutham, hitting him again and again on his behind. 'It's "Eat, my dear birdies", is it, young man? That's how you earn your sixpence a day keeping the birds off my crops!' He stopped at last. 'Here's your payment for today. Now, go home and don't let me ever see you on my fields again!'

Jude found his aunt at home, selling a loaf to a little girl.

'Why are you back so early?' the old woman demanded.

'Mr Troutham has sent me away because I let the birds eat a little bit. There are the last wages I shall ever earn!' Jude threw the sixpence tragically onto the table.

'Ah! Why didn't you go to Christminster with that schoolmaster of yours?'

Jude helped his aunt for the rest of the morning. Then he went into the village and asked a man where Christminster was.

'Over there, about twenty miles away.' The man pointed to the north-east, past Farmer Troutham's field.

Jude's curiosity increased. The railway had brought him from the south up to Marygreen, but he had never been north beyond it. Quietly, he went back down to Troutham's field and up the far side, to where the path joined the main road. To his surprise, he found he was looking down on miles of flat lowland.

Not far from the road stood a farm building known as the Brown House. Jude stopped when he noticed a ladder and two men repairing the roof.

'I want to know where Christminster is, please,' he said.

'It's out across there, past those trees.' One of the men pointed. 'You can see it on a clear day.'

'The best time to see it,' said the other man, looking in the same direction, 'is when the sun's going down, all flaming red. But you can't see it now. It's too cloudy.'

In the evening, when Jude passed the Brown House again on his way home, the ladder was still there though the men had gone. He climbed up it, prayed, and waited.

About quarter of an hour before sunset, the clouds thinned in the west. Jude looked to the north-east as the men had told him. There, now, he could see points of light. The air became clearer still. Now the points of light showed themselves as the windows and shiny wet roofs and **spires** of a city. It was Christminster!

The boy looked on and on, until suddenly the shine went and the city was hidden again. The sun had set.

Jude climbed quickly down the ladder and began to run towards Marygreen, trying not to think about ghosts.

*Jude went to the Brown House whenever he could and looked eagerly into the distance.*

## Chapter Two

From this time on, Jude went to the Brown House whenever he could and looked eagerly into the distance. One evening when he was there, a team of horses came slowly up the hill, pulling coal.

'Have you come from Christminster?' he asked the carter.

'No, not that far,' replied the carter pleasantly. He noticed the book of stories under the boy's arm. 'You couldn't understand the books they read in Christminster, young man,' he went on. 'It's all learning there, nothing but learning and religion! I'm talking of the college life, of course. As for music, there's beautiful music everywhere in Christminster. And the buildings, well! There's nothing like them anywhere in the world ...'

Jude walked home, deep in thought. 'Christminster is a city of light,' he said to himself. 'It's a place of learning and religion. It would just suit me.'

But how could he prepare himself for Christminster? He would start learning. Yes, he would learn Latin and Greek! But how could he get the right books?

At about this date, Phillotson sent for his piano and that gave Jude an idea. He wrote his hero a letter, asking him to get him some old grammar-books in Christminster; and he hid the letter inside the piano.

Every morning before his aunt was up, Jude then called at the village post office. At last, a packet arrived. He cut the string, opened the books – and discovered, to his horror, that every word of both Latin and Greek had to be individually learnt!

'I can't do it!' he cried. 'Why was I ever born?'

♦

Jude was now twelve years old. He quickly recovered from his disappointment over the grammar-books and began to make himself useful to his aunt. Her bakery grew, and they bought an old horse and cart. Jude used this horse and cart for delivering bread to cottages outside the village, and for studying his Latin and Greek at the same time.

At sixteen, he decided to concentrate on Christian studies. He read the New Testament in Greek; and on Sundays he visited all the local churches, translating anything he found in Latin.

He was as determined as ever to go to Christminster. But how could he support himself there while he studied? He had no income and no **trade**. Perhaps he could enter the building trade. The uncle he had never met, his cousin Susanna's father, did **ecclesiastical** metal work. Perhaps he, Jude, could do church work of some sort, too.

As soon as he had settled matters with his aunt, he went to the little market-town of Alfredston, on the main road north of the Brown House, and found work with a **stone-mason** there.

Jude now stayed in the town during the week, and walked the five miles back to Marygreen every Saturday. In this way, he reached and passed his nineteenth year.


## Chapter Three

One Saturday afternoon at this time, Jude was returning early to Marygreen with his basket of tools on his back. It was fine summer weather and he was feeling pleased with his progress.

'Now,' he said to himself as he wandered back past the village of Cresscombe, 'I must settle in Christminster where I can buy books more easily. I'll save money and get into a college. I might even become a leader of the Church ...'

'Ha-ha-ha!' The sound of girls' laughter came over the hedge, but Jude did not notice.

'At Christminster, I must master ecclesiastical history ...'

'Ha-ha-ha!'

'I can work hard. Christminster will be proud of me.'

Jude was still deep in his dream when something soft and cold hit him on the ear and fell at his feet. He looked down. It was part of a pig, the unmentionable part of a pig!

He looked over the hedge. There was a stream and a cottage with some pigs. Three young women were kneeling by the stream, washing lumps of meat in the running water.

'Thank you!' he said, as he wiped his face.

'I didn't throw it!' said one girl to her neighbour.

'Oh, Anny!' said the second.

'You didn't do it, oh no!' Jude said to the third. He was almost sure she was responsible.

'Shan't tell you.' The girl was dark-eyed, well-built, almost handsome.

Jude climbed over the hedge and the two met on a small bridge over the stream.

'Don't tell people it was I who threw it!' said the girl.

'How can I? I don't know your name.'

'Arabella Donn. I live here. My father sells pigs.'

They talked a little more, and a little more. Jude had never before looked at a woman as a woman. Now he looked from Arabella's eyes to her mouth, to her breast, to her round bare arms.

'You should see me on Sundays!' she said.

'I don't suppose I could? Tomorrow? Shall I call?'

'Yes.' The girl looked at him almost tenderly, and returned to the congratulations of her companions.

Jude, as he went on his way, breathed new air. Suddenly, his plans for reading, working and learning were pushed to one side. 'But it's only a bit of fun,' he said to himself.

♦

It was Sunday afternoon and Jude was in his room at his aunt's. He would not, he decided, go to meet the girl. He would read his Greek New Testament. He sat down at the table and, almost as soon, jumped up again. He could surely give up just one afternoon … In three minutes, he was out of the house in his best clothes and on his way down to Arabella Donn's, west of the Brown House.

A smell of pigs came from the back and a man called out in a business-like voice, 'Arabella! Your young man!'

Jude entered just as Arabella came downstairs in her Sunday best. She looked so handsome that he was glad he had come.

They walked up to the Brown House, but in his excitement Jude did not once look towards Christminster. This country girl in her Sunday dress had agreed to take a walk with him! Our student, our future leader of the Church, was quite overcome. The pair went on to Alfredston and, at Arabella's suggestion, had some beer at an **inn**.

It was getting dark when they started home, and they walked closer together. 'Take my arm,' said Jude, and Arabella took it, up to the shoulder.

13

As they climbed to the Brown House, she put her head on his shoulder. Jude took the hint and kissed her. When they were halfway up the hill, he kissed her again. They reached the top and he kissed her once more.

It was nine o'clock when they arrived at her home and later still when 'Arabella's young man' got back to Marygreen. In his room, the New Testament still lay open on the table in silent accusation.

♦

Jude left early next morning for his usual week in Alfredston. At the place where he had first kissed Arabella, he stopped and sighed. Six days before he could see her again!

A little later, Arabella came the same way with her two companions. She passed the place of the kiss without even noticing it.

'And what did he say next?'

'Then he said …' Arabella repeated some of Jude's tenderest words to her.

'You've made him care for you,' said the one called Anny.

'Yes,' answered Arabella in a low, hungry voice. 'But I want more than that. I want him to have me, to marry me!'

'Well, he's an honest countryman. You can get him if you go about it in the right way.'

'What's the right way?'

The other two girls looked at each other. 'She doesn't know! Though she's lived in a town!'

'How do you mean? Tell me a sure way to catch a man, as a husband.'

Arabella's companions looked at each other again, and laughed. Then one spoke quietly in her ear.

'Ah!' Arabella said slowly. 'I didn't think of that.'

'Lots of girls do it,' said Anny.

# Chapter Four

Every weekend that summer, Jude walked out with Arabella. He made no progress with his books – but neither did he make the sort of progress that Arabella wanted.

Suddenly, one Sunday morning, the girl said to her mother, 'There's a service at Fensworth church this evening. I want you and Father to walk to that.'

'What's going on tonight, then?'

'Nothing,' said Arabella. 'But he's shy, and he won't come in when you're here.'

In the afternoon, as usual, she met Jude. They walked on the high ground and the sound of church bells floated up from below. When the bells stopped, Arabella suggested that they went home.

'I won't come in, dear,' Jude said, as usual.

'They've gone to church,' she said. 'Now, you'll come in?'

'Certainly!'

They went indoors. Arabella took off her jacket and hat, and they sat down, close together.

'You may kiss my cheek,' she said softly.

'Your *cheek*!' protested Jude and reached towards her. There was a little struggle. He held her close.

'One proper kiss,' he said, 'and then I'll go.'

But Arabella had jumped up. 'You must find me first!' she cried and ran out of the room. It was now dark and her lover could not see. Then a laugh showed that she had rushed upstairs. Jude rushed up after her.

◆

In the next two months, the pair met constantly. Arabella seemed dissatisfied, always waiting, wondering.

Then, one evening, Jude told her that he was going away. 'It'll be better for both of us,' he said.

Arabella began to cry. 'But it's too late!'

'What! It wasn't your own hair?' asked Jude in sudden disgust.
'You've enough of your own, surely?' 'Enough for the country,'
Arabella said.

'What?' asked Jude, turning pale. 'You're not ...'

'Yes, and what shall I do if you leave me?'

'Oh, Arabella! You *know* I wouldn't leave you. I have almost no wages yet, and this ends my dream of Christminster – but certainly we'll marry, my dear. We must!'

That night, Jude went out alone and walked in the dark. He had to marry Arabella. So he must, he told himself, for his own peace of mind, think well of her.

♦

The marriage notice was sent out immediately. Jude's aunt made him a wedding-cake, saying it was the last thing she could do for the fool, and Arabella sent slices to her two friends, labelled 'In remembrance of good advice'.

On the wedding night, Jude took his wife to a lonely roadside cottage he had rented between the Brown House and Marygreen. In their own bedroom for the first time, Arabella unpinned a long tail of hair from her head and hung it on the mirror.

'What! It wasn't your own hair?' asked Jude in sudden disgust. 'You've enough of your own, surely?'

'Enough for the country,' she said. 'But in towns the men expect more. When I was a **barmaid** at Aldbrickham in North Wessex ...'

'False hair? A barmaid?' Jude turned away.

♦

The couple were poor. Jude was still just a nineteen-year-old **apprentice** stone-mason. He had rented the lonely cottage only so that Arabella could help by keeping a pig.

But Mrs Jude Fawley was pleased with her new position in life. She had a husband: that was the important thing. And he would be able to buy her new dresses when he threw away those stupid books and concentrated on his trade.

One day, in Alfredston, she met her friend Anny for the first time since the wedding.

'So it was a good plan, you see,' said the girl to the wife. 'And when do you expect ...?'

'Shhh! Not at all. I was mistaken.'

'Oh-ho, Arabella! "Mistaken"! That's clever! But he won't like it. He'll say it was a trick, a double trick.'

'Pooh! Anyway, what can he do about it? We're married now.' But Arabella did not look forward to telling Jude.

Then, one evening when he was tired after a hard day's work, he said as they went to bed, 'You'll soon have plenty of work yourself, dear, won't you?'

'How do you mean?'

'Well, I meant ... little clothes to make ... When will it be? Can't you tell me exactly yet?'

'There's nothing to tell. I made a mistake. Women get these things wrong sometimes.'

'Good God!' Jude lay down without another word.

When he woke up next morning, he seemed to see the world differently. But the marriage remained.


## Chapter Five

Winter came and, one Saturday at dawn, Jude and his wife killed the pig she had fattened. The killing troubled Jude – the animal's cries and Arabella's cruel ways.

'You tender-hearted fool!' she said.

Jude set off for his work. The road to Alfredston now reminded him too much of his first walks with Arabella, so he read as he walked, to keep his eyes down.

As he walked home that evening, he heard girls' voices behind a wall, just as he had once heard them behind a hedge.

'If I hadn't suggested it to her, she wouldn't be his wife today.'

'I think she knew there was nothing the matter when she told him she was ...'

The voices belonged to Arabella's old companions. They were talking about himself and her!

When Jude arrived home, Arabella was boiling up some fat from the pig. She wanted some money, she said. He ought to earn more. 'I don't know why you married, on your wages.'

'Arabella. That's unfair! You know why. Those friends of yours gave you bad advice.'

'What advice?'

Jude told her about the conversation he had heard.

'That was nothing.' Arabella laughed coldly. 'Every woman has the right to do that.'

'No, Bella. Not when it traps an honest man for life ... Why are you boiling up that fat tonight? Please don't.'

'Then I must do it tomorrow morning,' she said angrily.

Next morning, Arabella went back to her pig fat, still in a bad temper. 'So that's the story about me, is it? That I trapped you?' She saw some of Jude's books on the table and began throwing them to the floor.

'Leave my books alone! Your hands are covered in fat!' Jude caught her by the arms.

'That's right!' she cried. 'Make me work on a Sunday, then complain about it! Ill-use me as your father ill-used your mother, and as his sister ill-used her husband!'

Jude looked at her in amazement. He left her and went, after a while, to call on his aunt at Marygreen. 'Aunt,' he demanded, 'did my father ill-use my mother? Tell me.'

'I suppose that wife of yours has said something,' Drusilla Fawley replied. 'Well, there isn't much to tell. Your parents weren't happy together. Coming home from Alfredston market one day, they had their last quarrel and they separated on the hill by the Brown House. Your mother drowned herself soon after and your father took you away to South Wessex. His sister quarrelled with her husband too and went off to London with little Sue ... the Fawleys weren't made for marriage.'

Instead of returning to his own cottage, Jude walked to Alfredston where, at the same inn he had visited with Arabella, he drank for an hour or more. When he finally went home, laughing loudly and unsteady on his legs, he found a note from his wife: 'Have gone to my friends. Shall not return.'

Then a letter came. She was tired of him and their dull life, she said. She was leaving this stupid country. She was going to Australia with her parents.

Jude sent Arabella the money from the sale of their pig and everything else he had, and he went back into **lodgings** in Alfredston.

Eventually he heard of the family's departure for Australia and, the following evening, he walked by himself in the starlight, along the main road to the upland.

He felt like a boy again! But he was a man, he reminded himself, and a man who had separated from his wife. He came to the Brown House, where his own parents had separated and where he had first seen, or imagined, Christminster.

He looked to the north-east and saw, in the far distance, a ring of light. It was enough. He would go to Christminster, he decided, as soon as he finished his apprenticeship.

## PART TWO: AT CHRISTMINSTER

## Chapter Six

Three years after Arabella's departure, Jude finally arrived at Christminster. He was now a serious and strong-faced young stone-mason, black-haired with a black beard. He hoped to find work in the city of his dreams and was pleased that he had not only a friend there, the schoolmaster Phillotson, but also a relation. He had seen a photograph of a pretty girl at his aunt's and she had said that it was his cousin Sue Bridehead, who now lived somewhere in Christminster.

Jude arrived at sunset and got himself lodgings in a suburb known as Beersheba. Excited, he went straight out to explore the place he had dreamed of for so long.

It was a windy, whispering, moonless night. Alone in the darkness, he wandered along streets and down **obscure**, forgotten alleys. He saw the old colleges. He heard their bells. He felt their aged stonework with his mason's fingers. As the leaves brushed against their walls in the wind, he met the ghosts of the university's great men ...

Next morning, when Jude woke, the ghosts of the past had gone. He found a good job as a stone-mason and began earning and learning with enthusiasm, renewing the city's old stonework by day and studying his books by night. His whole aim was to enter the university. But, like most dreamers, he had no definite plan of action. He did, however, have the photograph of Sue. His aunt had sent it, but with a request that he would stay away from his Bridehead relations and not bring trouble into the family. Sue's father had gone to London, she added, but the girl was working as some sort of artist in a shop selling ecclesiastical objects.

Jude put up the photo in his room and felt, somehow, more at home. He walked past the ecclesiastical shops and saw, sitting behind a desk in one of them, a girl just like the one in the picture. She was doing some lettering on metal, so she must surely be his cousin, following her father's trade. Jude did not speak to her. His aunt had asked him not to. Besides, he was in his rough working-jacket – and she was so pretty! So he walked away and began day-dreaming about the girl instead.

A few weeks later, Jude saw her in the street, as he worked on the stonework of one of the colleges. She came so close that he turned shyly away, but of course she did not know him. She was light and slight, lovely, nervous, tender ...

From this moment, the emotion which had been building up in Jude since his lonely arrival in the city of his dreams,

*Jude saw Sue next at the 'high' Church of St Silas in Beersheba.
She was led by the elderly lady who employed her.*

began to centre on this girl. He knew that, despite his aunt's request, he would soon introduce himself. But he *must* think of her in just a family way, he told himself. He was, after all, a married man. And she was his cousin. And if Fawley marriages usually ended in sadness, a Fawley marriage between blood relations might end in something worse …

Jude saw her next at the 'high' Church of St Silas in Beersheba, where he was doing some work. She was led by the elderly lady who employed her and he did not dare to make himself known to her. Man cannot live by work alone, and Jude wanted someone to love. 'But it can't be!' he told himself. 'I already have a wife!'

As the days went by, however, he found himself thinking of Sue more instead of less. Indeed, he was always thinking of her.

# Chapter Seven

One afternoon at this time, a dark-haired girl walked into the place where Jude worked, lifting her skirts to avoid the stone-dust and asking for Mr Jude Fawley.

'Look,' said a man known as Uncle Joe, 'that's the daughter of that clever Bridehead man who did the ironwork at St Silas ten years ago and then went away to London.'

Jude was out, so the girl left a note for him. 'My dear cousin Jude,' she wrote, 'I have only just learnt that you are in Christminster. Why did you not let me know? I very much wanted to get to know you, but now I am probably going away ...'

A cold sweat spread over Jude. He wrote back immediately, arranging to meet her in the city that same evening.

'I'm sorry,' he began shyly as Sue walked up to him, 'that I didn't call on you.'

'Oh, I don't mind that.' The voice was silvery. Sue looked Jude up and down, curiously. 'You seem to know me more than I know you,' she added.

'Yes, I've seen you now and then.'

'But you didn't speak? And now I'm going away!'

'Yes. That's sad. I know hardly anyone else. Well, I do have one very old friend here somewhere. I wonder if you know of him, Mr Phillotson?'

'I've sent books to a Mr Richard Phillotson at Lumsdon. He's the village schoolmaster there.'

'Only a schoolmaster still!' Jude's face fell. If his hero had failed in his dream of university, how could he, Jude, ever succeed? 'Let's go and call on him,' he said.

So they walked to Lumsdon, where a knock brought Phillotson to the schoolhouse door. He was now forty-five years old. His face was thin and worn, like his clothes, and Jude's schoolboy admiration turned to sympathy.

'I don't remember you at all,' said the schoolmaster

doubtfully when Jude told him his name. 'You were one of my pupils, you say?'

'It was at Marygreen,' Jude replied.

'Yes, I was there a short time. And is this a pupil, too?'

'No, this is my cousin ... I wrote to you for some grammar-books, if you remember. And it was you who started me on that. On the morning you left Marygreen, you told me to try to go to university – it was the thing to do, you said.'

'I told you that?' Phillotson was surprised. 'I gave up the idea years ago.'

'I've never forgotten it,' said Jude. 'That's why I came to Christminster, and to see you tonight.'

'Come in,' said Phillotson, 'and your cousin, too.'

His visitors chatted pleasantly for a while, but they did not stay to supper. Sue lodged with her elderly employer and she had to be indoors before it was late.

'Why do you have to leave Christminster?' Jude asked her regretfully as they walked back. They had talked only on general subjects, and she had spoken to him only as to a friend, but this cousin of his was an amazement to him. She was so alive! Sometimes an exciting thought made her walk so fast that he could hardly keep up with her!

'I've quarrelled with Miss Fontover,' she said. 'I want some work in which I can be more independent.'

'Why don't you try teaching again? You taught in London once, you told Mr Phillotson. Let me ask him to have you at his school. If you like it and go on to a training college, you'll have twice as much income and freedom as any church artist employed by Miss Fontover!'

'Well, ask him. Goodbye, dear Jude. I'm so glad we've met at last. We needn't quarrel because our parents did, need we?'

How he agreed! Next day, he went to Lumsdon again and persuaded Phillotson to take on Sue Bridehead as a pupil-teacher.

♦

The schoolmaster sat in his little schoolhouse and looked at the cottage opposite. It was half-past eight in the morning and he was waiting to see Miss Bridehead come across the road for the morning's lessons.

She had been with him only for three or four weeks, but she was an excellent teacher, just as bright as Jude had described her. Already, he wished to keep her. Indeed, their work together had become a delight to him.

♦

Phillotson had invited Jude to walk out and see them that Friday evening. It was raining and Jude set off with a feeling of gloom. He knew now that he loved Sue, but he also knew that this love was wrong.

As he entered the village, he saw Sue and Phillotson walking along the empty road in front of him under one umbrella. Then he saw Phillotson put his arm round the girl's waist. Gently, she moved it away. Phillotson replaced it and this time, looking round her quickly and doubtfully, she let it remain. In horror, Jude sank back against the hedge out of sight; and the couple entered the school.

'Oh, he's too old for her – too old!' Jude cried hopelessly. But he could not interfere. Was he not Arabella's husband?

Unable to go on, he returned to Christminster. 'And it was I,' he said bitterly, 'who introduced them!'

## Chapter Eight

Jude's old aunt lay unwell at Marygreen, looked after by a neighbour, and that Sunday he went to see her.

'Was Sue born here?' he soon heard himself asking.

'In this room. So you've been seeing her!' said the old woman sharply.

'Yes.'

'Then don't! Her father brought her up to hate the Fawleys, and a town girl like that won't have any time for a working man like you.'

'But she's thoughtful and tender and — '

'Jude!' cried his aunt from her bed. 'It was bad enough for you to marry that woman Arabella. But it'll be even worse if you now go after Sue.'

The neighbour said she remembered Sue Bridehead at the village school, before she was taken to London. 'She was the smallest of them all,' said the Widow Edlin, 'but she could do things that only boys do usually. I've seen her slide with them on the ice in winter, with her little curls blowing. All boys except herself, and they used to cheer her! Then, suddenly, she used to run indoors and refuse to come out again ...'

Jude left his aunt's that evening with a heavy heart.

'You're at a college by now?' called out a villager.

'No.' Jude slapped his pocket meaningly, and walked on.

But the question brought him down to earth at last. 'All this waiting outside the walls of the colleges won't do!' he told himself as he journeyed back to Christminster. 'I must get proper information.'

So he wrote to the Masters of several colleges, asking for advice. As he waited for their replies, he heard news that Phillotson was leaving the Lumsdon school to go to a larger one further south. Was Sue involved? Was Phillotson wanting a bigger income for some reason to do with her? How could he now ask the schoolmaster's advice on his own situation?

Christminster, Jude realized, had had too powerful a grip on his imagination. It was not enough just to live there and study there. Without natural brilliance or proper teaching or a lot of money, he would never get into its university.

He always remembered the afternoon on which he awoke from his dream. He went high up into one of Christminster's many unusual buildings, a round theatre with windows that gave a view over the whole town. He looked down on all the colleges below – their spires, halls, churches, gardens – and saw, now, that they were not for him. His own future lay with the ordinary workers. Phillotson, he thought, must have had the same sort of disappointment. But Phillotson now had sweet Sue to cheer him.

That evening, one reply finally arrived from the Master of a college. 'Sir,' it said, 'I have read your letter with interest; and, judging from your description of yourself as a working man, I suggest that you will succeed better in life if you remain at your own trade …'

It was a hard blow after ten years of studying. Instead of reading as usual, Jude went down to the street, had a few glasses of beer at an inn and walked into town, looking for the real, ordinary Christminster.

◆

He did not go to his work next day. Again he looked for the real Christminster life. This time, he went to a low inn and sat there all day, drinking until his money had gone.

In the evening, the regular customers began to come in – Jude's fellow mason Uncle Joe, a man known as Tinker Taylor, an actor, two 'ladies', a couple of students … Jude, already drunk, said he was as good as any university Master and showed off his church Latin in return for another drink.

'*Credo in unum Deum, Patrem omnipotentem* …' Suddenly, he realized what he was doing. In self-disgust, he left the inn and went to the only person in the world who could help him.

'Sue! Sue!' Late in the evening, he knocked at the lighted window of her lodging opposite the Lumsdon school.

'Is it Jude? My dear, dear cousin, what's the matter?'

'I am so bad, Sue. My heart is nearly broken. I've been drinking and speaking against God and …'

She took him indoors, sat him down and pulled off his boots. 'Sleep now,' she said. 'I'll come down early in the morning and get you some breakfast.'

Jude woke at dawn. Ashamed and unable to face her, he left the house. Whatever could he do? He must get away to some obscure place and hide, perhaps pray. The only place he could think of was his aunt's. She had sold the bakery business now, so her cottage was quiet enough.

He called at his lodgings and found a note of **dismissal** from his employer. Jobless and moneyless, he packed his things and walked the twenty miles to Marygreen, sleeping one night in a field outside Alfredston.

'Out of work?' asked his aunt, looking at his clothes.

'Yes,' said Jude heavily. He went up to his old room and lay down, still dressed. When he woke up, he felt that he was in hell – the hell of failure, both in ambition and in love. He could hear his aunt praying in the next room and, not for the first time, he thought of entering the Church.

## PART THREE: AT MELCHESTER

## Chapter Nine

Jude did some little local jobs, putting up **headstones** on **graves**, and continued to think about the ecclesiastical life. A man could do good, he told himself, without going to the colleges of Christminster. He could enter the Church in a more modest way and spend his life in an obscure village, helping others. *That* might be true religion. The idea encouraged him, but he did nothing about it until a letter arrived from Sue. She was going to enter a teacher's training college, she wrote, at Melchester in Mid-Wessex.

There was a **theological** college at Melchester also! Jude could work in the city, study, join the theological college and be ready to enter the Church at the age of thirty …

♦

Christmas came and went. Sue was already at Melchester and Jude planned to go there in the spring. She had not once mentioned either his behaviour that night he arrived at her cottage or any involvement with Phillotson.

Suddenly, however, she sent for him. The college was even worse than the shop. Could Jude come immediately?

Her cousin packed up his things and left for Melchester with a lighter heart.

On his way from the station to see Sue, Jude paused under the walls of Melchester Cathedral. He looked up at its lovely spire and down at all the new stone lying on the ground. Here too, then, old stonework was being renewed and he might find exactly the employment he wanted.

As he came to the west front of the cathedral, a wave of warmth passed over him. Sue's college was opposite. That quick, bright-eyed girl with the pile of dark hair was here!

But the college was a college for young ladies, and the girl who came to greet him was different from before. She wore a plain, dark dress, her hair was twisted tightly up, her movements were quieter.

'I'm glad you've come!' Sue came prettily forwards, but there was no sign that she thought of Jude as a lover. He *must*, he said to himself, tell her about his marriage, but he did not want to.

The cousins walked into the town and Sue talked freely about everything except the subject that most interested Jude. When they sat for a while, he put his hand on hers. She smiled and looked coolly at his fingers. 'I like to see a man's hands rough from his work,' she said. '… Well, I'm glad I came to Melchester, after all. See how independent I shall be after the two years' training! And then Mr Phillotson will help to get me a big school.'

She had mentioned him at last. 'I was afraid,' said Jude, 'that perhaps he wanted to marry you.'

'Now don't be so silly! An old man like that!'

'Oh, come, Sue! I saw him putting his arm round your waist.'

Sue bit her lip. 'You'll be angry if I tell you everything … But I *shall* tell you,' she said, with the sudden change of mood that was part of her. 'I – I've promised to marry him when I finish at the college. We'll then take a large school together and have a good income between us.'

'Oh, Sue!' Jude turned away.

'I knew you'd be angry! We'd better not meet again.'

That was the one thing Jude could not face. 'I'm your cousin,' he said quickly. 'I can see you when I want to!'

'Then don't let's talk of it any more. What does it matter, anyway? It's not going to happen for two years!'

Jude could not understand her. 'Shall we go and sit in the cathedral?' he asked.

'Cathedral? I'd rather sit in the railway station,' she answered in annoyance. 'That's the centre of town life now. I'm tired of old things!'

'How modern you are, Sue!'

'I must go back,' she said, 'or I'll be locked out.'

Jude took her to the college gate and said good night. His drunken visit to her at Lumsdon, he thought, had led to this promise to marry Phillotson.

Next day, he found the employment he wanted, on the cathedral repairs. Having also found respectable lodgings close by, he bought books and began to study Theology.

## Chapter Ten

One Friday, a few weeks after Jude's arrival, Sue had an afternoon's leave. Where should they go? After some discussion, the pair went by train into the countryside and started to walk across high, open land to the next station.

In their excitement, however, they missed the last train back and had to stay the night in a lonely cottage.

'Are you a married couple?' the son of the house asked Jude privately.

'Shhh, no!'

'Then she can go into Mother's room, and you and I can lie in the outer room after they've gone through. I'll call you early enough to catch the first train back in the morning.'

'I expect I'll get into trouble,' Sue said.

◆

The following evening, Jude was studying at his lodgings when a stone was thrown lightly at his window.

'Jude! It's Sue! Can I come up without anyone seeing me?'

Jude's heart leapt. Had she come to him in trouble as he had once come to her?

In a moment, his cousin entered his room. 'I'm so cold!' she said. 'Can I sit by your fire?'

'Whatever have you done, darling?' He had not meant to call her that.

'They locked me up because I stayed out with you. It seemed so unfair. So I got out of the window and escaped across a stream!' She was trying hard to sound independent.

'Dear Sue!' Jude took her hand. 'But you're very wet! I'll borrow some clothes from the lady of the house.'

'No! Don't let her know! They'll find me!'

'Then you must put on some of mine.' Jude gave her his Sunday suit and left the room.

When he returned, she was asleep in his suit in his only armchair, with her own clothes spread out to dry. He stood with his back to the small fire, looking at her, loving her.

Then, saying he had 'a young gentleman visitor', he asked for supper in his room.

'Eat this,' he commanded when Sue woke up, 'and stay where you are. Tomorrow is Sunday. I can sit here by the fire all night and read. Don't be frightened.'

'I have no fear of men, as such, nor of their books,' she said thoughtfully. 'I have mixed with them almost as one of their own sex. When I was eighteen and in Christminster, I became friendly with one student in particular: he taught me a lot and lent me many books.'

'Has your friendship finished?'

'Yes. He died, poor man. But we used to go about together – on walking tours, reading tours – like two men almost. I agreed to live with him after he graduated. But when I joined him in London, I found that he meant a different thing from what I meant, and so after a time we separated. He said I was breaking his heart. My father was in London, but he wouldn't have me back, so I returned to Christminster.'

Jude's voice shook. 'However you've lived, Sue, I believe you're innocent.'

'I've never given myself to any lover, if that's what you mean!' she said.

'Have you told Mr Phillotson about this friend of yours?'

'Yes, long ago. He just said I was everything to him, whatever I did.' There was a silence. 'Are you very annoyed with me, dear Jude?' she suddenly asked in a voice of extraordinary tenderness. 'I care as much for you as for anybody I ever met.'

'But you don't care *more*!' There was another silence. 'I'm studying Theology now, you know,' Jude said, to change the subject. 'Would you like to say evening prayers with me?'

'I'd rather not,' she said. 'My friend taught me to have no respect for all that tradition ... But I won't upset your beliefs. Because we are going to be *very* nice with each other, aren't we?' She looked trustfully up at him.

Jude looked away. Was his heart going to be the next one that she broke? But she was so dear! If only he could forget her sex as she seemed able to forget his, what a companion she would make!

They talked on until Sue fell asleep again, deep inside his jacket. At six in the morning, when her clothes were dry, he touched her on the shoulder and went downstairs into the starlight.

When he returned, she was in her own clothes again. 'Things seem so different in the cold light of morning,' she said. 'I've run away from the college! Whatever will Mr Phillotson say? He's the only man in the world for whom I have any respect or fear ... Well, that doesn't matter, I shall do as I choose!' She would go a few miles away, she said, to a village near the town of Shaston, to stay with the sister of a fellow-student until the college allowed her back.

They went quietly out of the house towards the station, watched equally quietly by a woman at an upstairs window.

'I want to tell you something; two things,' Jude said quickly as the train came in.

'I know one of them,' Sue said, 'and you mustn't! You mustn't love me. You must only like me! Goodbye!'


## Chapter Eleven

Jude hated Melchester that Sunday, but next morning a letter arrived which changed everything.

'What a cruel and ungrateful woman I was at the station!' Sue wrote from the village near Shaston. '*If you want to love me, Jude, you may.*'

Jude wrote straight back, of course. Then, receiving no reply, he sent a message that he was coming out to see her the following Sunday.

He found her lying in bed. 'Sue, what's wrong?' he cried. 'You couldn't write?'

'They won't have me back at the college,' she answered. 'That's why I didn't write. Not the fact, but the reason! Somebody has sent them untrue reports – and they say you and I ought to marry as soon as possible, for the sake of my good

*33*

name! But I don't think of you as a lover. At least, I hadn't quite begun to. And I never supposed *you* loved *me* till the other evening. Oh, you've been so unkind, not telling me!'

'I'm to blame, Sue,' Jude said simply, 'more than you think.' He had meant to tell her about Arabella, but still he could not. 'You belong to Mr Phillotson,' was all he said. 'I suppose he's been to see you?'

'Yes,' she said after a short pause. 'Though I didn't ask him to.'

Jude left in the afternoon, hopelessly unhappy.

But the next morning, another note arrived from the village near Shaston. 'Jude, I'm coming to Melchester on Saturday to collect my things from the college. I could walk with you for half an hour if you like.'

Jude asked her to call for him at the cathedral works.

♦

At Shaston itself, a dozen miles from Melchester, a middle-aged man was dreaming a dream of great beauty about the writer of the above note. Richard Phillotson had recently returned to his native town, to run a large school and make preparations for taking a wife.

Sue Bridehead had written to him, too. Whenever he was away from his pupils, he read and re-read her short notes from Melchester, kissing them like a boy of eighteen. But why, he puzzled, did she not want him to visit her?

One Saturday morning, unable to keep away any longer, he went to call on her. It was two weeks after her sudden departure from the college, and Sue had told him nothing whatever about it. Shaken at the news the college now gave him, he entered the cathedral opposite – and saw Jude among the workmen inside.

Both men were embarrassed: Jude was expecting to see Sue that same day; Phillotson had just been told that Jude was Sue's lover.

'I hear,' said Phillotson, his eyes on the ground, 'that you have seen my little friend Sue recently. May I ask — ?'

'About her escape from the training college?' Jude readily explained the whole series of adventures.

'You're telling me,' said Phillotson as he finished, 'that the college's accusation is untrue?'

'It is,' said Jude. 'Absolutely. I swear it before God!'

♦

The schoolmaster left the cathedral at about eleven, but Sue did not appear and Jude finally found her in the market square.

'You haven't seen Mr Phillotson today?' he asked.

'I haven't – but I refuse to answer questions about him! I've already written and said that you may love me …'

Jude knew that, as an honest man, he must now tell her about Arabella.

'Why didn't you tell me before!' Sue burst out when he had finished. 'Before I could write that note!'

'But I never thought you cared for me at all, till quite recently, so I felt it didn't matter! *Do* you care about me, Sue?'

She chose not to answer the question. 'I suppose she – your wife – is a very pretty woman, even if she's bad?'

'She's pretty enough – but I've not seen her for years.'

'How strange of you to stay away from her like this,' said Sue shakily. 'You, so religious, unlike me!'

Jude tried to put an arm round her waist.

'No, no!' she said, with tears in her eyes. 'You can't mean that as a cousin; and it mustn't be in any other way.'

They walked on, and she recovered. 'What does it matter?' she smiled. 'We have to stay separate, anyway. We're cousins, and I'm promised to somebody else.'

'There was another reason why I didn't tell you everything,' said Jude. 'My great-aunt has always told me that I ought not to marry, that Fawley marriages end badly.'

'That's strange. My father used to say the same!'

They stopped and looked at each other.

35

'Oh, it can't mean anything,' said Sue lightly. 'Our family's been unlucky in marriage, that's all.'


## Chapter Twelve

Sue returned to her friend's house near Shaston and, a day or two later, a letter came from her.

'My dear Jude,' she wrote, 'Mr Phillotson and I are to be married in three or four weeks. You must wish me happiness! Your affectionate cousin, *Susanna Bridehead*.'

Jude twisted in pain. Then he laughed a bitter laugh and went off to work. 'Oh, Susanna!' he said to himself. 'You don't know what marriage means!' Could the story of his own marriage have made her agree to this now?

A second letter followed. 'Jude, will you give me away at my wedding? You are my only married relation in the area, and it seems from the Prayer Book that somebody has to "give me" to my husband, like a she-animal. I suppose you too, O Churchman, have this high view of woman! Ever, *Susanna Bridehead*.'

What a fool that 'married relation' made him seem as her lover! Bravely, Jude wrote back: 'My dear Sue, Of course I wish you happiness! And of course I will give you away. I suggest that you marry from my house since I am, as you say, your nearest relation. But I don't see why you sign your letter in such a distant way. Ever your affectionate, *Jude*.'

So it was all arranged. Jude moved into new and larger lodgings, away from the woman who had reported on his 'gentleman' visitor; and Sue came to stay in the same house.

They saw each other very little. Phillotson came frequently, usually when Jude was out. He would obviously be a kind and loving husband, but what did Sue feel? Jude was depressed that, having made a wrong marriage himself, he was now helping the woman he loved to do the same.

On the morning of the wedding, the cousins went for a last walk together.

'That's the church where you'll be married,' Jude said, pointing.

'Indeed? Let's go in!'

They entered by the western door. Sue held Jude's arm, almost as if she loved him.

'I shall walk through the church like this with my husband in about two hours,' she said a little later, her hand still on his arm. 'Was it like this when you were married?'

'Good God, Sue, don't be so pitiless!'

'Forgive me, Jude!' Her eyes were wetter than his.

Why did she do these things? Later, Jude wondered this again during the wedding service. Why had she asked him to give her away – and why had he ever agreed? She was nervous, he could see. As he gave her away to Phillotson, she could hardly control herself. And, as the newly-married couple departed, Sue looked back at Jude with fear in her eyes.


## Chapter Thirteen

She could not possibly go home with Phillotson! Surely she would return! Jude waited, but Sue did not come. He looked out of the window and imagined her journey to London, where they had gone for their holiday. He looked into the future and imagined her with children ...

His depression deepened in the following days. Then he heard that his aunt was seriously ill at Marygreen, and that his old employer at Christminster had a job for him.

He went first to Marygreen, from where he wrote to Sue at Shaston. If she wanted to see her Aunt Drusilla alive, he said, she should come up immediately by train. He would meet her tomorrow evening, Monday, at Alfredston station, after he had seen his old employer in Christminster.

◆

The City of Learning looked beautiful, but Jude had lost all feeling for it. The only ghost it held now was the ghost of Sue. Her chair was still there in the shop, empty.

He went to see his old employer, but could not bring himself to return to this place of lost dreams. He met Tinker Taylor and, in his depression, went with him to the inn where he had got so drunk before.

With nothing to do until his train left for Alfredston, Jude sat on alone behind one of the inn's glass screens. A barmaid served someone on the other side. Jude looked up, and was amazed to see that the barmaid was Arabella. Arabella, in a black dress with a white collar, chatting happily.

'Well, have you heard from your husband, my dear?' her customer asked.

'I left him in Australia,' she replied, 'and I suppose he's still there.' She gave the man his change and he caught at her hand. There was a little struggle, a little laugh, and the man left.

Jude hesitated, then went around the screen.

'Well!' Arabella recognized him with surprise. 'I thought you must have died years ago! Have a drink, for old times' sake!'

'No, thanks, Arabella,' Jude said without a smile. 'How long have you been here?'

'About six weeks. I returned from Sydney three months ago, and I saw this job in an advertisement.'

'Why did you return?'

'Oh, I had my reasons. You're not at the university or in the Church?'

'No ... ' Jude noticed a jewelled ring on her hand. 'So you tell people you have a living husband?'

'Yes. There might be problems if I called myself a widow. But we can't talk here. Can you come back at nine?'

'All right,' Jude said gloomily. 'I suppose we'd better arrange something.' He put down his unemptied glass and went out. He would not now be able to meet Sue at

Alfredston, but he had no choice. In the eye of the law and the Church, this woman was his wife.

When he returned to the inn at nine, it was crowded. The barmaids were pink-cheeked and excited. Arabella insisted on pouring a drink for Jude as well as another for herself.

'Until we've come to some agreement, we shouldn't be seen together here,' she said. 'Let's take the train to Aldbrickham. Nobody will know us there for one night.'

'As you wish.'

They made the half-hour's journey to Aldbrickham, and entered an inn near the station in time for a late supper.


## Chapter Fourteen

'You said when we were getting up this morning that you wished to tell me something.' Jude had just come back to Christminster on the train with Arabella.

'Two things,' she replied. 'One was about that gentleman I mentioned last night, who managed the Sydney hotel. You promise to keep this a secret?' She spoke unusually quickly. 'Well, he kept asking me to marry him, and at last I did.'

Jude turned pale. 'What – marry him? Legally, in church?'

'Yes. And I lived with him till we had a quarrel and I came back here. He talks of coming to England for me, poor man!'

'So that was the "husband" you talked of in the bar. Why didn't you tell me last night! Arabella, you've committed a crime!'

'Crime? Pooh! He was very fond of me and we lived as respectably as any other married couple out there. There was one more thing I wanted to tell you, but that can wait. I'll think over what you said about your circumstances, and let you know.'

Jude watched her disappear into the inn where she worked and turned back towards the station, burning with shame at the memory of the last twelve hours.

Suddenly, there in front of him, was Sue. 'Oh, Jude, I'm so glad to find you!'

Emotionally, they took each other's hand and walked on together, each conscious that this was their first meeting since Sue's marriage.

She had come to Christminster early this morning to look for him, she said. 'I thought that perhaps you were upset that I was married and not here as I used to be, so you'd gone drinking again to drown your feelings!'

'And you came to save me, like a good angel! No, dear, at least I wasn't doing that. But I'm sorry I didn't meet you at Alfredston last night, as I arranged. I had a sudden appointment here at nine o'clock.' Looking at his loved one, so sweet and rare, Jude became even more ashamed of the hours he had spent with Arabella.

'Then where did you stay last night?' Sue asked the question in perfect innocence.

'At an inn.' How could he possibly explain?

They got on the next train to Alfredston, talking a little stiffly. Jude could not forget that Sue was now 'Mrs Phillotson', though she seemed unchanged. She had been married less than a month but, both on the train and as they walked from Alfredston to Marygreen, she avoided all conversation about herself. Jude became sure she was unhappy.

When they reached the cottage beyond the Brown House where he had lived with Arabella, he heard himself saying: 'That's the house I brought my wife home to.'

Sue looked at it. 'That cottage was to you as the schoolhouse at Shaston is to me.'

'But I wasn't happy there as you are. If you *are* happy, Mrs Phillotson.'

'He's good to me!' Sue burst out. 'If you think I'm not happy because he's too old for me, then you're wrong.'

Jude said no more. They walked down into the field where Farmer Troutham had beaten him as a boy, up the other side to the village – and found Mrs Edlin at their aunt's door.

'She's got out of bed!' she cried. 'I couldn't stop her!'

They entered and saw Drusilla Fawley sitting, wrapped in blankets, by the fire.

'You'll regret this marrying, too!' she screamed at Sue. 'And why that schoolmaster, of all men? You can't love him!'

Sue ran out, and Jude found her crying in the old bakehouse. 'It's true!' she said.

'God – you don't like him?'

'I don't mean that,' she said quickly. 'But perhaps I was wrong to marry.' Then she dried her eyes and said, as she left for Shaston, that Jude must not come to see her, not yet.

♦

Jude stayed on at his aunt's, studying his Theology and trying desperately to forget his love for Sue.

While he was there, a letter arrived from Arabella. Her Australian husband had come to London, she wrote, and wanted her to run an inn with him in Lambeth. He said he still loved her, and she felt she belonged to him more than to Jude, so she had just gone to join him. She wished Jude goodbye and hoped he would not inform against her.

Then, on the Thursday before Easter, when Jude had returned to Melchester, a note came from Sue. She was now teaching at her husband's school, she said, and of course Jude must visit them. He could come that afternoon if he wished.

## PART FOUR: AT SHASTON

## Chapter Fifteen

Jude climbed up from the station to the hilltop town of Shaston and found the schoolroom empty. Mr Phillotson was away at a meeting, said a girl cleaning the floor, but Mrs Phillotson would be back in a few minutes.

There was a piano in the room, the same piano that

Phillotson had had at Marygreen. Jude, as he waited, played a tune he had heard at a church in Melchester.

Lightly, someone touched his left hand. 'I like that tune,' said Sue, 'I learnt it at the training college.'

'Then you play it for me.'

Sue sat down and played. When she had finished, they again touched hands. 'I wonder why we did that?' she said.

'I suppose because we two are in tune!'

'We'll have some tea,' Sue said quickly. 'Are you still studying Theology?'

'Yes, harder than ever.'

'I could come and see you at one of your churches next week.'

'No. Don't come!'

'What have I done? I thought we two —'

'Sue, I sometimes think you're playing with my affections,' Jude said angrily.

She jumped up. 'Oh, Jude, that was a cruel thing to say! Some women need love so much, and they may not always be able to give their love to the person licensed by the Church to receive it! But you're too straight to understand … Now you must go. I'm sorry my husband's not at home.'

'Are you?' Jude went out.

'Jude! Jude!' Sue called pitifully from the window. 'I'm really all alone! Come and see me again. Come next week.'

'All right,' said Jude.

◆

Two days later, Sue changed her mind. 'Don't come next week,' she wrote to Jude. 'We were too free. You must try to forget me.'

'You're right,' Jude wrote back. 'It's a lesson I ought to learn at this Easter season.'

Their decisions seemed final, but on Easter Monday Drusilla Fawley died and it was necessary for Jude to inform

*'What have I done? I thought we two—'*
*'Sue, I sometimes think you're playing with my affections,' Jude said angrily.*

Sue. 'Aunt Drusilla is dead,' he wrote from Marygreen. 'She will be buried on Friday afternoon.'

Sue came, alone and nervous, and the cousins went together to the burial service.

'She was always against marriage, wasn't she?' asked Sue afterwards, when they were back at the familiar cottage.

'Yes. Particularly for members of our family.'

Sue looked at Jude. 'Would a woman be very bad, do you think, if she didn't like living with her husband just because she had, well, a physical feeling against it?'

Jude looked away. 'Sue, you're not happy in your marriage, are you?'

'Of course I am! … But I have to go back by the six o'clock train.'

'That train won't take you to Shaston. You'll have to stay

here until tomorrow. Mrs Edlin has a room if you don't wish to stay in this house.'

Sue's hand lay on the tea-table. Jude put his hand on it, but Sue took hers away. 'That's silly, Sue!' he cried. 'It was a totally innocent action!'

'Then I must tell Richard that you hold my hand,' she said. 'Unless you are sure that you mean it only as my cousin?'

'Absolutely sure. I have no feelings of love now.'

'Oh! How has that happened?'

'I saw Arabella when I was at Christminster.'

'So she's come back and you never told me! I suppose you'll live with her now?'

'Of course – just as you live with your husband.'

There were tears in Sue's eyes. 'How could your heart go back to Arabella so soon?... But I must be as honest with you as you've been with me. Though I like Mr Phillotson as a friend, I hate living with him as a husband! There, now I've told you.' She bent her face down onto her hands and cried until the little table shook.

'I *thought* there was something wrong, Sue.'

'There's nothing wrong, except the awful contract to give myself to this man whenever he wishes. *He* does nothing wrong, except that he has become a little cold since he found out my feelings. That's why he didn't come today. Oh, I'm so unhappy! Don't come near me, Jude. You mustn't!'

But Jude had jumped up and put his face against hers. 'It all happened because I was married before we met, didn't it? That's the only reason you became *his* wife, Sue, isn't it?'

Instead of replying, Sue left the house and went across to Mrs Edlin's cottage.

◆

Next morning, Jude walked with Sue as far as the main road to Alfredston. He must not kiss her goodbye, she said, unless he promised that he kissed her only as a cousin and friend.

No, he would not promise that. So they separated. But then both looked round at the same time – and ran back into each other's arms, kissing close and long.

The kiss was a turning-point for Jude. To him, it seemed the purest moment of his life, but to his Church it would seem nothing of the sort. He realized that he could not possibly continue in his unlicensed love for Sue *and* hope to become a teacher of religion.

That evening, he lit a fire in the garden and calmly put all his theological books on the flames.


## Chapter Sixteen

Phillotson met his troubled wife at the station and tried to interest her. His schoolmaster friend Gillingham had called for the first time since their marriage, he said, and —

'Richard, I let Mr Fawley hold my hand. Was that wrong?'

'I hope it pleased him,' was all Phillotson said.

Sue did not mention the kiss. That evening, she went to bed early, saying she was tired. Her husband worked on school matters and did not go to their room until nearly midnight. Sue was not there.

'I'm not sleepy now. I'm reading by the fire.' Her voice came from the back of the house, near the kitchen.

Phillotson went to bed, but when he woke up some time later, she was still not there. He went downstairs. 'Sue?'

'Yes.' The voice, very small, now seemed to come from a clothes-cupboard under the stairs.

'Whatever are you doing in there? There's no bed, no air!' He pulled at the door. Sue was lying on some cushions in her white night-dress.

'Oh, please, go away!' She knelt, wide-eyed and pitiful.

'But I've been kind to you and given you every freedom. It's awful that you feel this way!'

'Yes, I know,' she said, crying. 'Life is so cruel!'

'Shhh! The servant will hear. I hate such odd behaviour, Sue. You give in too much to your feelings.' And so he left her, only advising her not to shut the door too tightly.

At breakfast the next morning, Sue asked her husband to let her live away from him. 'Will you let me go? Will you?'

'But we married, Susanna.'

'We made a contract. Surely we can unmake it? Then we could be friends, and meet without pain. Richard, have pity!'

'But you promised to love me.'

'It's foolish to promise always to love one person!'

'And does "living away" from me mean living by yourself?'

'Well, if you insisted, yes. But I meant living with Jude.'

'As his wife?'

'As I choose.'

Phillotson gripped the table. 'I can't allow you to go and live with your lover. We would lose everyone's respect.'

'Then allow me to live in your house in a separate way.'

To that, finally, the schoolmaster agreed. He watched his pretty wife teaching in his school, and felt very lonely.

◆

Phillotson kept his promise and moved to a room on the other side of the house. But then, one night, he absent-mindedly entered their old room and began to undress. There was a cry from the bed and a quick movement towards the window. Sue leapt out.

In horror, he ran down and gathered up in his arms the white shape lying on the ground.

Sue was, in fact, scarcely hurt. 'I was asleep, I think!' she began, turning her pale face away from him. 'And something frightened me – a terrible dream. I thought I saw you — '

Sick at heart, Phillotson watched her go slowly upstairs. He sat with his head in his hands for a long, long time. Then, next day after school, he walked down to the little town of Leddenton and knocked at the door of his old friend, Gillingham.

♦

'Now, George, when a woman jumps out of a window and doesn't care whether she breaks her neck or not, the meaning is clear. And so I'm going to do as she asks.'

'What, Dick, you'll let her go?' Gillingham was amazed. 'And with her lover?'

'I shall. I can't defend my decision religiously or any other way, but I think I'm doing wrong to refuse her … I had no idea that simply taking a woman to church and putting a ring on her finger could involve one in such a daily tragedy! I shall let her go.'

'But with a lover!'

'She hasn't definitely said she'll live with him as a wife. And it's not just animal feeling between the two: I think their affection will last. One day, in the first jealous weeks of my marriage, I heard them talking together at the school. There was an extraordinary sympathy between the pair …'

'But what about family life? What about neighbours, society? Good God, what will Shaston say?' Gillingham walked to the door with his friend, 'Stick to her!' were his final words.

Next morning, Phillotson told Sue that he agreed to her departure. Only he did not wish to hear, he said, anything about Jude Fawley or about where she was going.

Having made the decision, he felt a new sense of peace.


## Chapter Seventeen

Sue left Shaston one evening after dark, taking with her only one small trunk. Phillotson put her on the station bus, then returned to the schoolhouse and packed away all her remaining things.

Jude met her at Melchester station, carrying a black bag and looking handsome in his Sunday suit. His eyes shone with love. 'There wasn't time to tell you, dear one,' he said, getting onto the train. 'We can't stay here, where we're known. I've given up my cathedral work. We're going on to Aldbrickham. I've booked a room for us at a hotel.'

'One room? Oh, Jude, I didn't mean that!' Seeing his shock, Sue put her face against his cheek. 'Don't be angry, dear. Perhaps I *am* free to live with you from this moment, but Richard has been so generous and if I loved him ever so little as a wife, I'd go back to him even now ... But I don't love him.'

'And you don't love me either, I half fear. Sue, I sometimes think you are incapable of real love.'

Sue moved away from him, looking out into the darkness. 'My liking for you is not as some women's, perhaps,' she said in a hurt voice. 'But I do love to be with you. I've let you kiss me and that tells enough.'

Jude sat back, remembering the poor Christminster graduate. Then he forgave her, as he always did, and they sat side by side with joined hands. 'You know you're all the world to me, Sue,' he said gently, 'whatever you do.'

It was about ten o'clock when they reached Aldbrickham. Sue would not go to the hotel, so a boy wheeled their luggage to the George Inn, where they took two rooms.

'Your relation came here once before, late just like this, with his wife,' said a maid chatting to Sue. 'About a month or two ago. A big, handsome woman.'

Sue was quiet throughout supper. 'You came here lately with Arabella,' she accused Jude as they went upstairs afterwards.

Jude looked round him. 'Why, yes, it is the same place! I really didn't know it, Sue.'

'When were you here? Tell me!'

'The day before you and I met in Christminster and we went back to Marygreen together. I told you I had met her again.'

'But you didn't tell me everything. You've been false to me!'

She was so upset that Jude had to take her into her room.

'But, Sue, you had a new husband and she was my legal wife —'

'Was it this room? Yes, I see by your face that it was!'

Sue buried her face in the bed. 'I thought you cared for nobody in the world except me!'

'It's true. I did not, and I don't now,' said Jude.

'I thought that a separation – like yours from her and mine from him – ended a marriage.'

'I don't want to speak against Arabella, but I must tell you one thing which settles the matter. She has married another man! I knew nothing about it until after she and I came here. And now she's asked me for a **divorce**, so that she can remarry this man legally. So I'm not likely to see her again.'

Sue got up. 'Then I forgive you. And you may kiss me just once, here, on my cheek. You do care for me very much, don't you, in spite of my not – you know?'

'Yes, sweet,' Jude said with a sigh. 'Good night.'


## Chapter Eighteen

'Shaston' soon began to talk about Sue's absence. A month after she left, Phillotson was questioned about it by the school governors and he was too honest to lie. 'She asked my permission to go away with her lover, and I gave it,' he told them. 'Why shouldn't I? She wasn't my prisoner.'

But he had young people in his care! He must not appear to encourage such behaviour! Consider the effect on the town!

The governors asked Phillotson to leave the school. Against his friend Gillingham's advice, he refused. So they dismissed him, and that led to an illness. Day after day, the schoolmaster lay in his bed: a middle-aged man, facing failure and sadness.

Gillingham came to see him and, after a time, mentioned Sue's name. 'Where are she and her lover living?' he asked.

'At Melchester, I suppose. That's where he was.'

Gillingham then wrote Sue an unsigned note, addressing the envelope to Jude. From Melchester, the note was sent on to Marygreen, from where Mrs Edlin sent it to Aldbrickham.

Three days later, the sick man heard a little knock at his bedroom door.

Sue entered, as light as a ghost. 'I heard that you were ill,' she said, 'and as I know that you recognize other feelings between man and woman than physical love, I've come.'

The amazed servant-girl brought up tea; and Phillotson and his wife talked of this and that. Sue had heard no news from Shaston and so he simply told her that he was leaving the school. He was not seriously ill, he said.

Sue went to the window. 'It's such a beautiful sunset, Richard,' she said thoughtfully.

'Is it? It doesn't shine into this dark corner.'

'I'll help you to see it,' she said, and moved a mirror to a place by the window where it caught the sunshine. 'There – you can see the great red sun now!'

Phillotson smiled sadly at her child-like kindness. 'You *are* an odd little thing!' he said, as the sun glowed in his eyes. 'To come and see me after what has happened!'

'I must go home now,' she said quickly. 'Jude doesn't know where I am.' She went to the door, and he noticed tears on her face.

'Sue!' He had not meant to call her back. 'Do you wish to stay? I'll forgive you everything.'

'Oh, you can't!' she said. 'Jude is getting a divorce from his wife, Arabella.'

'His wife! It's news to me that he has a wife.'

'It was a bad marriage. But he's divorcing her as a kindness because she wants to remarry. I *must* go now.' Sue's fear had returned, and she did not tell her husband that she was still not living with Jude as a wife.

'She's his, from lips to toe!' said Phillotson as she left.

Next time Gillingham came, Phillotson seemed better. He told his friend about Sue's visit and said that he had decided, in kindness, to divorce her.

'Freedom will give her a chance of happiness,' he said. 'Because then they'll be able to marry.'

## Chapter Nineteen

The following year, Sue and Jude were still living separately, in a little house in Spring Street, Aldbrickham, that was rented by Jude. A sign on the door said, 'Jude Fawley: Mason'. He now made headstones, cheaply, for which Sue marked out the letters.

One Sunday morning in February, at breakfast, Sue held up an envelope. The courts, she said as Jude kissed her, had agreed to her divorce from Phillotson. Jude's divorce had come through a month before. 'But I feel that I got *my* freedom under false pretences,' Sue worried. 'If the courts had known the truth about you and me, they would not have given Richard the divorce.'

Jude had to smile. 'Well, you have only yourself to blame for the false pretences, darling!'

His happiness at their new freedom made Sue happier too. She suggested that they should go into the countryside for a walk, and she put on a bright dress to celebrate.

'So, my dear, we can marry at last,' Jude said as they made their way towards the wintry fields.

'I suppose we can,' said Sue without enthusiasm. 'But I have the same old fear of a marriage contract. Remember our parents! I might begin to be afraid of you, dear Jude, when you had a Government licence to love me!'

'My own sweet love, I don't want to force you into anything! For the rest of our walk, we'll talk only about the weather.'

◆

One Friday evening at the end of that month, there was a knock at the front door. Jude opened his window and saw a woman under the street-light.

'Is that Mr Fawley?' The voice was Arabella's!

'Whatever do you want, Arabella?'

Sue came into Jude's room, immediately upset.

'I'm sorry to call so late, Jude,' Arabella said, 'but I'm in trouble.' Her man hadn't married her after all, she went on, and she had a sudden responsibility that had arrived from Australia. If Jude could walk with her towards the Prince Inn where she was staying for the night, she would explain.

'Don't, don't go tonight, dear!' Sue was shaking. 'She only does it to trap you again. She's such a low sort of woman – I can see it in her shape, and hear it in her voice!'

'I shall go,' said Jude. 'God knows I love her little enough now, but I don't want to be cruel.' He moved towards the stairs.

'But she's not your wife!' cried Sue wildly. 'And I —'

'And you're not either, dear, yet,' said Jude. 'I've waited with patience, but we're living here in one house, both of us free, and *still* you will not be mine!'

Sue was now crying as if her heart would break. 'Very well then, I will be. Only I didn't mean to! And I didn't want to marry again! But I do love you.' She ran across and threw her arms round his neck. 'I give in!'

'And so I'll arrange for our marriage.'

'Yes, Jude.'

'Then I'll let her go,' he said softly. 'Don't cry any more. There, there and there.' He kissed Sue on one side, and on the other, and in the middle – and closed the window.

♦

The next morning was wet.

'Now, dear,' said Jude happily. 'I'll take along the marriage notice so that it can be made public tomorrow.'

'I was so selfish about Arabella!' said Sue. 'Perhaps she really did have a problem. Perhaps I should go and see her?'

'Arabella can look after herself,' said Jude calmly. 'Still, go to the inn if you want to. And then we'll take the marriage notice together.'

Sue went off under an umbrella, letting Jude kiss her and returning his kisses in a way she had never done before. 'The little bird is caught at last!' she said with a sad smile.

At the inn, saying she was a friend from Spring Street, Sue was asked to go upstairs. She found Arabella still in bed. 'I've just looked in to see if you're all right,' she said gently.

'Oh!' Arabella was disappointed. 'I thought my visitor was your friend, your husband – Mrs Fawley, as I suppose you call yourself?'

'Indeed I don't,' said Sue stiffly. She looked at Arabella's tail of hair hanging on the mirror and at the rain, and felt depressed.

Just then a maid brought in a telegram for 'Mrs Cartlett'. Arabella read it and brightened. 'From Lambeth!' she said. 'My man agrees to keep his promise to marry me again. I sent him a telegram saying I'd almost got together with Jude again, and that frightened him! Well, I don't need Jude now, so I advise you, my dear, to persuade him to marry you as soon as possible.'

'He's waiting to, particularly since last night —' Sue went pink.

'So my visit helped it on – ha-ha!' laughed Arabella. 'Go on, let him marry you! Then, if he throws you out, the law will protect you; and if he leaves you, you'll have the furniture.' She put her hand on Sue's arm. 'I really did want Jude's advice on a little business matter. I'll write to him from London.'

When Sue reached home, Jude was waiting at the door. But she persuaded him not to take the marriage notice, not yet. Arabella, she said, had made her feel more than ever that legal marriage was a trap to catch a man.

'Sue, you're beginning to frighten me off marriage too! All right, let's go in and think about it.'


## Chapter Twenty

Three weeks later, while they were still thinking about it, a newspaper and a letter arrived from Arabella.

The newspaper, which Sue opened, reported the marriage of 'Cartlett–Donn' in Lambeth. 'Well, at least we don't have to worry about her now,' said Sue easily.

But Jude's attention was on the letter. 'Listen to this! "… The fact is, Jude, that a son was born of our marriage eight months after I left you, when I was at Sydney with my parents. They have looked after him ever since, but now they say they are sending him over to me. So I must ask you to take him when he arrives, because Cartlett might not like him. I swear he is your lawful son. *Arabella Cartlett*".'

Sue's eyes filled with tears.

'It *may* be true,' Jude said. 'But does it really matter whether a child is one's own by blood?'

At this, Sue jumped up and kissed Jude. 'We'll have him here, dearest! And if he isn't yours, all the better!'

'… Just imagine his life in a Lambeth drinking-house, with a mother who doesn't want him. The boy – my boy, perhaps – might start asking, "Why was I ever born?"'

'Oh, no, Jude! We must have him. I'll be a mother to him.'

So Jude wrote straight back, telling Arabella to send the boy on to them – and they agreed to marry before he came.

◆

The next evening, a small pale child knocked at the door of the house in Spring Street. Arabella had postponed writing to Jude until the ship from Australia was due; and the boy reached London Docks on the same day as she received Jude's answer. So she gave him a good meal, a little money, and put him on the next train to Aldbrickham, before Cartlett could see him.

Hearing the knock, Sue came down from her room.

'Is this where Father, Mr Fawley, lives?' asked the child.

Sue looked at him and ran to fetch Jude, who picked him up with a sad tenderness.

'Arabella's speaking the truth!' Sue burst out. 'I see you in him!'

The boy looked across at her. 'Are you my real mother at last? Can I call you Mother?' He began to cry.

'Yes, if you wish, my poor dear.' Sue put her cheek against his to hide her own tears. 'I do want to be a mother to this child,' she said to Jude after they had put him to bed, 'and marriage might make it easier. Oh, Jude, you'll still love me afterwards, won't you?'

♦

The boy was very quiet and serious. People called him Little Father Time, he said, because he looked so old.

His father was disappointed that he was not called Jude. 'We'll have him properly named in church,' he said to Sue, 'the day we're married.'

The morning after his arrival, they took their marriage notice to the district office. But they did not marry. They could not make themselves do it, either at the office or in church, even though the Widow Edlin arrived for the wedding.

'Don't tell the child,' Sue told her. 'We've only postponed it. And if Jude and I are happy as we are, what does it matter?'

## Chapter Twenty-One

One day in June of that year, two trains arrived at the little town of Stoke Barehills, bringing visitors to the Great Wessex Agricultural Show. One train came from Aldbrickham. The other came from London and, among the crowd that got off it, were a well-built, rather red-faced woman in city clothes and a short, rather top-heavy man with a round stomach.

'Heavens, Cartlett!' cried the woman, looking at a couple coming off the other platform. 'There's Jude Fawley!'

'They seem fond of one another and of their child.'

'It isn't *their* child!' said Arabella jealously. 'They haven't

*Jude and Sue walked on into the show-ground, enjoying their holiday and trying hard to make Father Time enjoy himself, too.*

been married long enough!' But Cartlett thought her child was still in Australia, so she said no more.

Jude and Sue walked on into the show-ground, enjoying their holiday and trying hard to make Father Time enjoy himself, too. Sue, in a new summer dress, holding up her white cotton sun-umbrella, was as light as a bird. Jude looked proud of her. Their delight in each other was obvious. They seemed like two halves of a single whole.

Arabella stayed close behind them. 'They can't be married,' she said, 'or they wouldn't be so much in love! See how — '

Cartlett lost interest and went off to the beer tent.

'Arabella!' She was greeted with a laugh by her girlhood friend Anny, who had come down for the day from Alfredston.

'Have you seen Jude and his young woman, or wife, or whatever she is?' said Arabella. 'There they are, by the horses!'

'She's pretty,' said Anny. 'He's nice-looking, too. Why didn't you stick to him, Arabella?'

'Yes, why didn't I?' She noticed Jude's hand reaching out to Sue's as the lovers stood close together.

'Happy?' Jude asked Sue, and Sue nodded.

'Silly fools — like two children!' Arabella said gloomily. She left them admiring some roses and went to join Cartlett, who was sitting at the bar, drinking and talking to one of the barmaids. 'Surely you didn't come fifty miles from your own bar just to stick in another?' she remarked, ready for a quarrel. 'Take me round the show as other men take their wives!'

## Chapter Twenty-Two

Arabella was not the only person who took an interest in Jude and Sue. When Father Time suddenly arrived, their neighbours began to talk about them. And when the child was called 'Jude' and sent to school, the pupils made hurtful remarks.

So the pair went off for several days 'to London'; and when

57

they came back, they let people understand that they were legally married at last. Sue, who had been called Mrs Bridehead, now openly took the name of Mrs Fawley.

But it was all too secret, too late. People began to avoid them and to give fewer orders for headstones. In the autumn, when Sue was expecting a child of her own, the couple were even dismissed from a lettering job in a local church.

Jude decided then to give up the house and look for work elsewhere. 'We'll have a better chance where we're not known,' he said to Sue. 'I'm sickened by ecclesiastical work now. Perhaps if I went back to baking, our way of life would matter less to people!'

And so they left Aldbrickham. Jude did no more church work. He now had few religious beliefs left and he did not want to earn money from people who disliked his ways. But he accepted other employment as a stone-mason wherever he found it; and, for the next two-and-a-half years, he and his growing family lived all over Wessex.

## Chapter Twenty-Three

On a Saturday afternoon in May, almost three years after she saw Jude and Sue at the agricultural show, Arabella came to the busy town of Kennetbridge, a dozen miles south of Marygreen. Anny drove the horse and cart in which she came, and the two friends agreed to meet again in half an hour.

Arabella, all in black, walked around Kennetbridge market on her own, and stopped in surprise at a little bakery counter run by a young woman and an old-faced boy. 'Mrs Fawley!'

Sue recognized her and changed colour. 'How are you, Mrs Cartlett?' she said stiffly. Then, seeing Arabella's black clothes, she became sympathetic. 'Oh! You've lost — '

'My poor husband, yes. He died suddenly six weeks ago. I'm living at Alfredston with my friend Anny ... And you, my little old man, I suppose you don't know me?'

'You're the woman I thought at first was my mother.'

Sue quickly sent the boy off with a basket of cakes to sell. 'He doesn't know yet,' she said. 'Jude's going to tell him when he's a little older.'

'Then you're living with Jude still? Married?'

'Yes.'

'Any children?'

'Two.' Sue hesitated.

'And another coming soon, I see. But why are you selling cakes now?' Unasked, Arabella took one and ate it. 'Jude used to be too proud a man for this.'

Sue bit her lip. 'My husband hasn't been well since he caught cold last winter, putting up some stonework for a music-hall in the rain. So now he makes these cakes, which he can do indoors. We call them Christminster cakes.'

'He still keeps on about Christminster then! But why,' Arabella's questioning continued, 'don't you go back to school-teaching? Because of the divorce?'

'That and other things. We gave up all ambition and were never so happy in our lives until Jude became ill.'

'Here's the boy again,' said Arabella. 'My boy and Jude's!'

♦

'Anny, I've heard of Jude again and seen *her*!' Arabella and Anny were driving back to Alfredston. 'I want him back!'

'Fight against it,' said Anny. 'He belongs to someone else.'

They drove on in silence across the upland until they saw the cottage where Arabella had once lived with Jude.

'He's more mine than hers,' Arabella burst out. 'I'd take him from her if I could!'

'Arabella! Your husband's only been dead six weeks!'

At the top of the hill by the Brown House, they gave a lift to a thin, elderly-looking man.

Arabella looked at him when he was in the cart, and looked again. 'Mr Phillotson?' she asked.

'Yes,' said the traveller politely. 'And you are —?'

'I was one of your pupils. Arabella Donn. I used to walk up from Cresscombe to your school at Marygreen ... And I married Jude Fawley, one of your night-school pupils.'

'*You* were Fawley's wife?' Phillotson lost his stiffness. He had recently returned to Marygreen, he said. It was the only school which would take him after his wife left him as she did.

Arabella told him that she had just seen Sue at Kennetbridge. 'She's not doing well. Her husband is ill and she's worried ... You were wrong to divorce her.'

'No,' said Phillotson. 'I'm sure that I was right.'

'She was innocent. The divorce was wrongly given. I talked to her just afterwards and I'm sure of it.'

He gripped the side of the cart. 'But she wanted to go.'

'Yes. But you shouldn't have let her.'

◆

When Sue had sold all the Christminster cakes, she and the boy left the market with their empty baskets and walked to some old cottages with gardens and fruit-trees. The Widow Edlin came to the door of one, carrying a baby and holding a little girl by the hand.

Jude was sitting inside, in an armchair. 'You've sold them all?' he asked, a smile crossing his thin, pale face.

'Yes.' Sue told him about the market. Then, when they were alone, she kissed him and told him about Arabella.

'Arabella at Alfredston!' Jude looked worried. 'Perhaps it's a good thing that we've almost decided to move on. I'll be well enough to leave very soon. Then Mrs Edlin can go home again – dear, faithful, old Mrs Edlin!'

He had so far avoided all the old places, he said, but now he would like to go back to Christminster if Sue agreed. 'What does it matter if we're known there? It's still the centre of the world to me because of my early dream. I'd like to go back to live there, perhaps to die there! I'd like to be there by a particular day in June ...'

## Chapter Twenty-Four

They arrived at Christminster on Remembrance Day, the day chosen by Jude.

'Let's go and watch the celebrations,' said Jude suddenly. 'We'll leave our luggage at the station and get lodgings later.'

He carried their baby son, Sue led their little daughter and Arabella's boy walked silently beside them until they arrived at a round theatre – the theatre from which Jude had looked out on the day he awoke from his Christminster dream.

Today, there were holiday crowds lining the open space between the theatre and the nearest college. 'Here's the best place! Here's where they'll pass!' cried Jude in excitement. He pushed his way close to the barrier, holding the baby in his arms. Graduates in red and black arrived at the college. The sky turned dark and it began to rain and thunder.

'It seems like Judgement Day!' whispered Father Time.

Jude would not leave. He explained details of the stonework to the people around him. Tinker Taylor and the stone-mason Uncle Joe called out to him. He spoke loudly to the crowd of his failure to enter the university.

'He does look ill and worn-out,' said a woman.

'I may do some good before I'm dead,' Jude went on, 'as a terrible example of what *not* to do — '

'Don't say that!' whispered Sue in tears. 'You've struggled so hard!' It was raining heavily now. 'Let's go on, dear. We haven't any lodgings, and you're not well yet.'

But Jude watched and waited until all the university doctors had walked across to the theatre. 'Well, I'm an outsider to the end of my days!' he sighed at last. 'But how pale you are, Sue!'

'I saw Richard among the crowd, and I felt afraid...'

'You're tired. Oh, I forgot, darling! We'll go at once.'

# Chapter Twenty-Five

Lodgings were difficult to find so late in the day. Eventually, a woman said she could take Sue and the children for a week if Jude could stay elsewhere.

But when Jude had left to collect their luggage and find lodgings for himself at an inn, Sue heard the woman's husband shouting downstairs. Then the woman came up and said they would have to leave tomorrow. Her husband, she said, wanted no children in the house.

The boy was deeply upset. 'Mother, what shall we do?'

'I don't know. I'm afraid this will trouble your father, but we won't tell him tonight.'

'It's all because of us children, isn't it?'

'Well, people do dislike children sometimes.'

'If children are so much trouble, why do people have them? I was a trouble in Australia and I'm a trouble here. Why was I ever born? When children are born that are not wanted, they should be killed straight away.'

She hesitated. Then she decided to be honest. 'There's going to be another baby in our family soon,' she said.

'What!' The boy jumped up wildly. 'Oh, Mother, you've never sent for another! Why couldn't you wait until we've more money and Father's well?' He burst into tears.

'Forgive me, little Jude,' she begged him, crying too. 'I'll explain when you're older.'

'I won't forgive you, ever, ever! I'll never believe you love me or Father or any of us any more!'

He ran into the next little room, where a bed had been spread on the floor for the three children. 'If we children weren't here, there'd be no trouble!' she heard him say.

'Go to sleep now, dear!' she commanded.

◆

Sue woke early next morning and she ran across to the inn, to tell Jude about the problem with the lodgings. They had a quick meal and then returned together to prepare the children's breakfast. All was still quiet in the children's little room and, at half-past eight, Sue went in to call them.

Jude heard a scream and saw her fall to the floor, unconscious. He ran forward, then looked down at the children's bed. It was empty. He looked round the room – and saw two little bodies hanging from the back of the door, like clothes, and the boy's body hanging from the ceiling.

In horror, he cut them down, laid Sue on her bed and ran for a doctor. But it was too late. The children had been hanging for more than an hour and all three were dead. 'Done because we are too many,' said a note in little Jude's writing.

Sue was conscious again but, at the sight of the note, her nerves gave way completely. Screaming and struggling, she was carried downstairs. She lay there, shaking and staring at the ceiling.

As soon as she could speak, she told Jude about her conversation with the boy the evening before. That must have caused the tragedy, she said. She was to blame.

'No,' said Jude, 'it was in his nature to do it, to wish not to live.' Then he too broke down.

'Oh, oh, my babies!' Sue cried. 'They had done no harm. Why were they taken, not I? We loved each other too much, too selfishly, you and I, Jude; and now we're punished ...'

◆

She had to stay on at the now-hated lodgings. People came and went – police, lawyers, newspaper men. The law took its course.

At last, the children could be buried. But then Sue tried to stop the grave-digger from covering the grave with earth. 'I want to see them once more,' she cried. 'Oh, Jude, please, Jude, I want to see them! Just one little minute ...'

Later that night, the child Sue was expecting was born dead.

# Chapter Twenty-Six

Sue hoped for death for herself too, but slowly she recovered. Jude returned to his old trade of stone-mason, and they moved to Beersheba, not far from the church of St Silas.

They talked endlessly that summer of their life together and of Life itself. Gradually, Jude realized that they had mentally travelled in opposite directions since the tragedy. Sue was no longer the fearless, independent thinker she had been. 'It's no use fighting against God,' she said. 'I must give up my selfish ways.' While Jude rarely went to church now, she went frequently to St Silas.

Finally, one Sunday evening when she returned from a service there, she told Jude that she did not ever want to marry him. 'And, dear Jude, I don't think I ought to live as your wife any more.'

'What! But you *are* my wife, Sue, in all except law.'

'I'm Richard's wife,' she said. 'I feel more and more sure that I belong to him, or to nobody.'

♦

A few evenings later, Arabella called at the lodgings, behaving correctly but looking poorer than before.

'Thank you for writing,' she said. 'I've just come from the child's grave. As it's your trade, Jude, you'll be able to put up a handsome headstone ... If he had been with me, perhaps it wouldn't have happened. But of course I didn't wish to take him from your wife.'

'I'm not his wife,' said Sue, and left the room.

'Why did she say that?' asked Arabella in a changed voice. 'She *is* your wife, isn't she? She once told me so.'

'I cannot tell you,' said Jude firmly.

'Ah, I see! Well, I thought I should call before I go back to Alfredston. Father has just come back from Australia. I'm living with him now. Mother died out there.'

As soon as she left, Jude looked for Sue. She was not in the house. He went to St Silas and found her lying there, in her black clothes, crying.

'I wanted to be alone,' she said, almost sharply. 'Why did you come?'

'Why?' he repeated, wounded to the heart. 'I, who love you better than my own self! Why did *you* come here, alone?'

'I felt so unhappy when Arabella came. She seems to be your wife still and Richard to be my husband. God has taken my babies from me to show me this. Arabella's child killed mine. That was God's judgement – the right killing the wrong.'

'This is terrible!' Jude replied. 'If your religion does this to you, then I hate it ... Come home with me, dearest.'

He lifted her up, but she preferred to walk without his support and she stopped at a little coffee-house. 'Jude,' she said, 'will you get yourself lodgings here?'

'I will – if you really wish. But *do* you?' He took her home and followed her up to the door of their room. She put her hand in his and said, 'Good night, Jude'.

'You have never loved me as I love you!' he burst out.

'At first, Jude, I admit, I just wanted you to love me. But then I couldn't let you go – possibly to Arabella again – and so I began to love you. And now I love you as much as ever. But I mustn't love you any more. I joined myself to Richard for life.'

'Oh, Sue!' Jude suddenly sensed his own danger. 'I'm a weak man! Don't leave me just to save yourself!'

'I'll pray for you, Jude, night and day.'

'I mustn't stay? Not just once more, as it has been so many times? Oh, Sue, my wife, why not? ... Very well. Perhaps it's all been my fault. Perhaps I spoilt one of the purest loves that ever existed between man and woman!' He went to the bed and threw one of its pair of pillows to the floor. 'Good night,' he said and started to go.

'This breaks my heart,' she said, her face wet with tears. 'Oh, kiss me!'

He took her in his arms and covered her tears with kisses.

'We'll see each other sometimes, won't we, Jude?' she said, freeing herself. 'We'll be dear friends just the same?'

Jude turned and went down the stairs.


## Chapter Twenty-Seven

The man whom Sue now thought of as her husband still lived at Marygreen. He had seen her on Remembrance Day at Christminster. Then he had read in the newspaper about the tragedy, and had puzzled at the age of the eldest boy.

A few weeks later, Phillotson was at Alfredston for the Saturday market and he met Arabella. She told him that the eldest boy had been her son, and that Sue was not, after all, married to Jude. 'And now, I hear, she doesn't live with him any more. She says she's your wife in the eyes of God.'

'Indeed? Separated, have they?'

'Yes. As for me, I hope soon to be in a bar again at Christminster or some other big town.'

Phillotson asked for Sue's address. Arabella gave it and walked on, smiling to herself.

The schoolmaster still wanted Sue in his strange way. He could remarry her, he thought, on the respectable excuse that he had divorced her wrongly. Then society might accept him again.

So he wrote to Sue, suggesting that she should return to him. It was a careful letter. Physical love, he wrote, had little to do with the matter. He simply wished to make their lives less of a failure.

◆

One evening soon after, Sue walked to Jude's new lodgings

*Jude turned on her fiercely. 'But you're my wife!' he shouted. 'I loved you, and you loved me, and we made our own contract.*

and told him that she was going to remarry Phillotson.

Jude turned on her fiercely. 'But you're *my* wife!' he shouted. 'I loved you, and you loved me, and we made our own contract. We still love each other. I *know* it, Sue!'

'But I'm going to marry him again,' she answered, 'at the Marygreen church. And you should take back Arabella.'

'Good God, what next? What if you and I had married legally?'

'I'd have felt just the same.'

Jude shook his head hopelessly. Had the tragedy destroyed her reason? 'Wrong, all wrong! You don't love him.'

'I admit it. But I shall try to learn to, by obeying him.'

Jude argued and begged, but she was unshakeable. 'I didn't think you'd be so rough with me,' she said. 'I was going to ask you —'

'To give you away?'

'No. To come to the children's grave with me.'

So they went to the grave, and there they said goodbye.

◆

The next day was a Friday. Sue left Christminster alone, having asked Phillotson not to come for her. She wanted to return to him freely, she said, just as she had freely left him.

She sent her luggage on in front of her and walked the last half mile into Marygreen in the early evening. 'I've come, Richard,' she said, looking pale and sinking into a chair in the new schoolhouse. 'Will you take me back?'

'Darling Susanna.' He bent and kissed her cheek – and Sue moved nervously away. 'So you still dislike me!'

'Oh no, dear! I'm cold and wet from the journey, that's all. When is our wedding?'

'Tomorrow morning early, I thought. But it's not too late to refuse if you —'

'I want it done quickly.'

'Well, my friend Gillingham has already come up from Shaston to help us. Join us for supper and then I'll take you over to your room at Mrs Edlin's.'

◆

Morning came. A thick fog had moved up from the lowland and drifted by the trees on the village green covering them with big drops. At half-past eight, before many people were around, Sue and Phillotson were remarried.

Later in the day, Phillotson walked out a little way to say goodbye to Gillingham. Sue seemed nervous when he got back. 'Of course, my dear,' he said, 'I shall allow you to live just as privately as before.'

Sue brightened a little.

# Chapter Twenty-Eight

The following evening, a woman in black stood on the doorstep of Jude's lodgings in the rain. 'Father's turned me out after borrowing all my money for his new business! Can you take me in, Jude, while I look for work?'

'No!' said Jude coldly. But Arabella cried, and finally he agreed to let her use a little room at the top of the house for a few days.

'You've heard the news, I suppose?' she said then. 'Anny writes that the wedding was arranged for yesterday.'

'I don't want to talk about it.'

At first, Arabella did not come near Jude. But, the next Sunday, she asked if she could join him for breakfast as she had broken her teapot.

They sat for a while in silence. Then she said that she could find out about the wedding if he wanted to know. She needed to go to Alfredston to see Anny – and Anny had relations at Marygreen.

Hating himself, Jude agreed. He paid for her journey and, impatiently, met her at the station in the evening.

'They're married,' she smiled. 'Mrs Edlin said Sue was so upset that she even burnt the prettiest things she'd worn with you. Still,' Arabella sighed, 'she feels that he's her only husband in the eyes of God.' She sighed again. 'I feel exactly the same!'

Jude left her without a word. In his depression, he walked to all the places in the city he had visited with Sue. Then he turned into an inn.

Hours later, Arabella went to the inn where she had once worked as a barmaid and, as she expected, found Jude sitting there, half drunk.

'I've come to look after you, dear boy. You're not well.' Arabella suddenly seemed to have some money again. She bought him more drinks, stronger drinks. And whenever Jude said, 'I don't care what happens to me,' she replied, 'But I do, very much!'

When closing time came, she guided him out onto the street. 'You can't go back to your lodgings in this condition. Come round to my father's. He's more friendly towards me now.'

'Anything, anywhere,' said Jude. 'What does it matter?'

And so she guided him to her father's new little pork-and-sausage shop, her arm around his waist and his arm, at last, through unsteadiness, around her.

'This way,' she said in the dark, after she had shut the door. 'I'll pull off your boots,' she whispered. 'Now, hold on to me. First stair, second stair, that's it ...'

◆

Arabella looked at Jude's curly black hair and beard on the white pillow next morning, and felt well pleased.

'I've got a prize upstairs!' she told her father down in the shop. 'It's Jude. He's come back to me.'

She went off to Jude's lodgings and, unasked, brought away all his things and her own. Then, 'to advertise Father's new shop', she invited people like Uncle Joe and Tinker Taylor from the inn to a party. And, all the time, she kept Jude so drunk that he did not know where he was or what he did.

On the fourth day, in front of all the party guests, she said, 'Come along then, old darling, as you promised.'

'When did I promise anything?' asked Jude.

Arabella looked at her father. 'Now, Mr Fawley,' said Donn, 'you and my daughter have been living here together on the understanding that you were going to marry her.'

'If that's so,' said Jude hotly, standing up, 'then by God I *will* marry her!'

'Don't go,' Arabella said to the guests. 'We'll all have a good, strong cup of tea when we come back.'

'I like a woman that a breath of wind won't blow down,' said Tinker Taylor after the three had left for the church. 'Mrs Fawley, I suppose?' he said when they returned.

'Certainly,' said Arabella smoothly, pulling off her glove and holding out her left hand.

'She *said* I ought to marry you again,' said Jude thickly. 'True religion! Ha-ha-ha! Give me some more to drink!'

## Chapter Twenty-Nine

After their remarriage, Jude and his wife moved to new lodgings nearer the centre of the city. At first, Jude was able to work, but by the autumn he was a sick man again.

'Why can't you stay healthy?' complained Arabella, as he coughed and coughed. 'Soon I'll have to sell sausages out on the street to support you!'

Jude laughed bitterly. 'I've been thinking of that pig you and I once had. I tried to finish it off as quickly as possible. If only someone would now do the same for me!'

He did not get any better, and one day he begged Arabella to write and tell Sue. 'You know I love her, and I'd like to see her once more. I've one foot in the grave, so what can it matter?'

'I won't have that loose woman in my house!'

Jude leapt up from his chair, forcing Arabella back onto a sofa. 'Say anything like that again and I'll kill you!'

'Kill me?' she laughed. 'You couldn't even kill that pig properly!'

Jude began to cough and had to let her go. But one morning soon afterwards, in heavy wind and rain, he left the house when she was out and went to the station.

Wrapped in a long coat and blanket, pale as a ghost, he travelled by train to Alfredston and from there he walked the five miles to Marygreen. At half-past three, he stood by the familiar well. He crossed the green, asked a boy to fetch Mrs Phillotson from the schoolhouse, and entered the church.

There was a light footstep. 'Oh, Jude, I didn't know it was you!' Sue tried to go back, but he begged her not to. 'Why did you come?' she asked, tears running down her face. 'I know – it was in the Alfredston newspaper – that you've done the right thing and married Arabella again.'

'God above, "the right thing"? It's the worst thing of my life, this contract with Arabella! *You're* my wife. How could you go back to Phillotson?'

'He's a kind husband to me. And I've struggled and prayed and I've nearly made myself accept him. You mustn't wake —'

'Oh, you darling little fool! Where has all that intelligence gone, that fighting spirit?'

'You insult me, Jude. Go away!' She turned.

'I will. Sue, you're not worth a man's love.'

She turned back. 'Don't! Kiss me, oh, kiss me, and say I'm not a coward!' She rushed to him. 'I must tell you, my darling love! My remarriage has been a marriage in name only. Richard himself suggested it.'

'Sue!' Pressing her to him, Jude hurt her mouth with kisses. 'I have a moment's happiness now. You do love me still?'

'You know it! But I *mustn't* kiss you back … And you look so ill — '

'So do you! There's one more kiss, in memory of our dead children, yours and mine.'

The words struck Sue like a blow. 'I *can't* go on with this … But there, darling, I give you back your kisses. I do, I do!'

'I ask you one last time. We were both out of our senses when we remarried. Let's run away together!'

'No; again, no! Why do you tempt me, Jude? Don't follow me, don't look at me. Leave me, for pity's sake!'

Sue ran to the east end of the church and knelt there. Jude picked up his blanket and went straight out, coughing. Sue hesitated, then put her hands over her ears. At the corner of the green, by the path to Farmer Troutham's old field, Jude looked back at Marygreen for the last time. Then he walked on.

When a cold wind is blowing, the coldest place in all Wessex is the top of the hill by the Brown House. Here Jude

*Jude picked up his blanket and went straight out, coughing. Sue hesitated, then put her hands over her ears.*

now walked, wet through, against a bitter, north-east wind. It was ten o'clock when he finally reached Christminster.

Arabella was waiting on the platform. 'You've been to see her?'

'I have. I've got my only two remaining wishes in the world: I've seen her and I've finished myself.'

All the way back to their lodgings, Jude saw the same ghosts of great men that he had seen on his first arrival at Christminster. 'They seem to be laughing at me now. But, Arabella, when I'm dead, you'll see my ghost among these!'

'Pooh! Come along and I'll buy you something warm to drink.'

◆

While Jude and Arabella were walking home, Sue was talking to Mrs Edlin in the schoolhouse. 'I've done wrong today, Mrs Edlin. Jude has been here and I find that I still love him … I'll never see him again, but I must now make things right with my husband. I shall go to his room tonight.'

'I wouldn't, my dear. He agrees to separate rooms, and it's gone on very well for three months as it is.'

'Yes, but I was wrong to accept the arrangement … Don't go, Mrs Edlin!' Sue begged nervously. 'Please stay in my room tonight.'

They went up the stairs together. Sue undressed in her own room. Then, with a frightened look at the widow, she crossed to her husband's room and half-opened the door.

'Is that you, Susanna?'

'Yes, Richard.' She almost sank to the floor. 'I've come to beg your pardon and ask you to let me in.'

'You know what it means?' Phillotson said firmly.

'Yes. I belong to you. Please let me in.'

Mrs Edlin closed the door of Sue's old room and got into bed. 'Poor little thing!' she said. 'How it blows and rains!'

◆

After Christmas, Jude again lay ill at home.

'You were clever,' said Arabella, 'to get yourself a nurse by marrying me! I suppose you want to see your Sue?'

'No. Don't tell her that I'm ill. Let her go!'

One day, however, Mrs Edlin came to see him. Arabella left the old woman alone with Jude, and he immediately asked about Sue. 'I suppose,' he said bluntly, 'they are still husband and wife in name only?'

Mrs Edlin hesitated. 'Well, no. It's been different since the day you came. She insisted. To punish herself.'

'Oh no, my Sue! ... Mrs Edlin, she was once a woman who shone like a star. Then tragedy hit us, and she broke. Our ideas were fifty years too soon, and they brought disaster on us both!' Jude cursed the world angrily, and then began to cough.

## Chapter Thirty

Summer came round again and, with it, the Remembrance celebrations. Jude lay on his bed, very sick.

One afternoon, while the bells rang out, Arabella sat waiting for her father to take her place as nurse. He did not come. She looked impatiently at Jude. He was asleep. So she went out anyway, to join the crowds.

It was a warm, cloudless day. The sound of concert music reached Jude's room as his cough started and woke him. 'A little water, please,' he said, his eyes still closed. 'Some water – Arabella – Sue – darling! Please! ' No water came. 'Oh, God,' Jude whispered, 'why was I ever born?'

When Arabella returned, she was met outside by two or three of the stone-masons. 'We're going down to the river for the Remembrance games,' said Uncle Joe. 'But we've called on our way to ask how your husband is.'

'He's sleeping nicely, thank you,' said Arabella.

'Then why not come along with us for half an hour, Mrs Fawley? It would do you good.'

'I *wish* I could. Well, wait a minute. Father is with him, I believe, so I can probably come.'

She ran upstairs. Her father had not arrived, but Jude seemed to be sleeping, although he lay strangely still. Arabella went close to the bed. His face was quite white. His fingers were cold. She listened at his chest. His heart, after nearly thirty years, had stopped.

The happy rum-tum-tum of a band reached her ears from the river. 'Why did he die just now!' said Arabella, annoyed.

She thought for a moment. Then she softly closed the bedroom door again and went off with the men to the river.

'Oh, I'm glad I came!' she said, looking at all the boats and flags and people. 'And my absence can't hurt my husband.' A man she knew put his arm around her waist, and she pretended not to notice. 'Well, it's been good,' she cried later, when all the excitement was over. 'Now I must get back to my poor husband.'

By ten o'clock that night, Jude's body was laid out on the bed. Through the half-open window, the sound of dance music entered from one of the colleges.

◆

Two days later, two women stood looking down at Jude's face as the sounds of Remembrance Day itself came into the room from the round theatre.

'How beautiful he is!' said Mrs Edlin, red-eyed.

'Yes, handsome,' agreed Arabella. 'Do you think *she*'ll come?'

'I don't know. She swore not to see him again! Poor heart! She looks years and years older.'

'If Jude had seen her again, perhaps he wouldn't have cared for her any more … But he told me not to send for her.'

'Well, the poor little thing *says* she's found peace.'

'She may swear that on her knees,' said Arabella, 'but it's not true. She'll never find peace again until she's where he is now!'

# EXERCISES

## Vocabulary Work

Look back at the 'Dictionary Words' in this book. Check that you know the meaning of all the words.

1 Choose the right word for each phrase below.

*divorce    dismissal    obscure    apprentice    cart*
*graves    lodgings    stone-mason    trade*

a A wheeled vehicle, for carrying people or luggage.
b A person who can decorate a building with stone.
c The rooms you rent to live in.
d The opposite of marriage.
e A job you learn to earn a living, especially with your hands.
f A person learning a trade.
g Dead people are buried here.
h Losing your job; being sent away.
i Difficult to see; hard to understand.

2 Use your dictionary to help you answer these questions.

a What would you study at a *theological* college?
b What would you read on a *headstone*?
c What would you buy from a *baker*?
d What would a *barmaid* sell you?
e What could you do at an *inn*?
f What would you find at the bottom of a *well*?
g Where would you usually find *cottages*?
h Where do people do *ecclesiastical* work?
i Where would you see *spires*?
j Where do *hedges* grow?

## Comprehension

*Chapters 1–5*

1 Why does Jude want to live at Christminster?
2 Why does he marry Arabella?

*Chapters 6–8*

  3 Who does Jude want to find in Christminster?

  4 How does he try to show he is as clever as a university man?

*Chapters 9–14*

  5 What warning does Jude's great-aunt give him about marriage?

  6 Where did Arabella go after she left Jude?

*Chapters 15–18*

  7 Why is Sue so unhappy?

  8 What crime did Arabella commit in Australia?

*Chapters 19–25*

  9 Why won't Sue marry Jude?

10 Why does little Jude kill himself and the other children?

*Chapters 26–30*

11 How do the children's deaths affect Sue?

12 How old is Jude when he dies?

13 Here are six statements about events in the book, marked a–f.
   Copy the map and put the right letter in each circle to show where
   each thing happened.

   a Jude lived here with his great-aunt as a little boy.

   b This is where Jude learnt to be a stone-mason.

   c This was the city of Jude's dreams!

   d He first saw Christminster from here.

   e Phillotson and Sue ran a school here.

   f Sue did her teacher-training at college here.

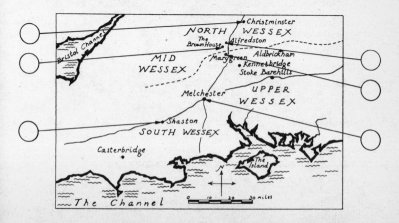

## Discussion

1 'Obscure' can mean 'not well known' or 'difficult to understand.' In what ways was Jude Fawley 'obscure'?

2 'Well, I'm an outsider to the end of my days!' says Jude. What made Jude an 'outsider'? Society? The Law? His personality? Or was it written in the stars when he was born?

## Writing

1 Read Chapter 6 again. Imagine you are Jude's Aunt Drusilla and write the letter you send him with Sue's photo (100 words).

2 Pretend you are Jude. Write to your Aunt Drusilla telling her about the ways in which Sue has changed after the deaths of the children, and asking her advice.

## Review

1 Do you think the tragic events in this book are the result of bad luck or bad judgement? Why?

2 This book was so heavily criticized when it was first published that Hardy decided not to write any more novels. What is it about the characters' behaviour that brought such strong criticism then? Would *you* criticize it for the same reasons today?